SINGLE DAD IN STUDIO 7D

MARYANN CLARKE

E-book ISBN: 978-1-988743-28-8
Print ISBN: 978-1-988743-06-6

Cover illustration ©Elle_Maxwell

Want to read the Latest Book in the LIFE is a JOURNEY Series?
Pre-Order A Forged Affair Now mybook.to/Forged
Want to connect with me?
www.maryannclarkescott.com
maryann@maryannclarkescott.com

If you enjoy reading this book, please rate it and leave a review on Goodreads HERE. Your opinion can make or break an author's success, and it means the world to me.
Click here to leave a review: https://www.goodreads.com/book/show/45285118-single-dad-in-studio-7d

CHAPTER ONE

"Namaste," said Lucy Clough at the end of her class, her palms pressed together, her head bowed in genuine thanks for the opportunity to pay her debt to Grandpa Henry. Short-term deprivation was a small price to pay for all he'd done for her, and, she hoped, would free her from the guilt that anchored her life in the past instead of the future.

"Thanks Lucy," said Anna. "See you Thursday," she added as she bounced out the door. Lucy was glad Anna came here to do yoga. Otherwise she'd miss her friend and workmate while she was away.

"If you haven't prepaid," Lucy said to everyone else, "you can leave your payment in the tray on the kitchen counter. See you Wednesday." She stood and ticked names off her list as a few people dropped cash onto the lacquer tray on their way out.

Lucy closed the door after her last student departed, then set to rearranging her studio for the rest of her workday. She sprayed the yoga mats and blocks and neatly re-folded blankets and tucked them onto the wooden shelves under the wide bench along the back window wall. She stood a moment studying the flaking white-painted brick wall across the back lane and sighed.

Then she counted out the money. So far she was just getting by. A few more clients or an extra class in her schedule might give her more comfort financially. But an extra class would cut into her precious research time and make her task that much harder. And the studio, perfect as it was, could accommodate only one or two more students per class without overcrowding.

She'd just have to keep her costs low and make this work. Her deadline was only a few precious weeks away. Once she'd achieved her goal, she could return to her regular job at the university and the money begin to flow again. Along with the rest of her life. Maybe once she'd put to rest the sense of outstanding debt, or was it was honour, to Grandpa Henry and his life, then maybe she could get unstuck and tackle her other life goals.

The vague items on her own life list: career advancement, travel, love, family maybe, she'd not given too much thought in the past few years. Ever since Grandpa's health took a sharp turn for the worse, she'd felt guilt over spending time on herself instead of him when he'd needed her most. At first, when was diagnosed with Alzheimer's, she promised herself she'd spend time with him, helping him to write his memoirs, working to capture the memories before they faded forever. But finishing grad school had robbed them both of the opportunity, and now someone else would steal Grandpa's ideas and his legacy would fade into oblivion along with his memories.

Arms akimbo, she turned to the large hulk of a screen that sectioned off her studio, and sighed. She needed an easy way to move the stupid thing back and forth every day. She had picked it up from a junk and antique shop on Main Street, but it weighed a ton. It was in fact a vintage freestanding chalkboard from a mid-century classroom, that she'd draped with inexpensive sari fabric from a shop in Little India. It did the trick of transforming her cluttered workspace into a serene and zen-like yoga studio twice each day.

As she shoved it inch by inch away from her worktable and against the opposite wall to give herself some elbow-room, its heavy wooden frame squeak, squeak, squeaking along the wooden floor, she knew she had to get wheels or gliders on the feet, and soon. Before her neighbours complained and she lost this once-in-a-lifetime opportunity.

Lucy turned and surveyed the large room. The opportunity to sublet this space for the next few months filled her chest with warmth. A friend had told her about this building. It was a unique live-work artists' studio complex. Considering how many sorts of people lived and ran their businesses from here, it ought to be a more common type of housing. It fit her needs to a T.

From what she could tell in the past week since she'd moved in, and begun running her yoga classes, she'd noticed signs for artists, designers, and wellness practitioners like herself. Even a day-care for kids. If she were a career yoga teacher, this would be a great opportunity long term.

But, in her case, it was a short-term sublet that suited her perfectly. The regular tenant Zahra's travel plans aligned with Lucy's sabbatical from her research job at the university, giving her this window to complete her research on her grandfather's work on a tight budget. But it was a one-shot deal. If she couldn't review his journals, notes, and photos, and pull together a coherent story, before her time was up, her efforts would be in vain.

She'd have to return to work, Peter Sinnehausser would publish his book, take credit for everything, and any claims she made on her grandfather's behalf afterwards would leave a distinct flavour of vinegar. And forever after, her grandfather's lifetime of research would be lost to the world, along with his legacy. She couldn't let that happen.

JEAN PHILIPPE ROCHE woke with a start when he heard the now-familiar noise. Squeak, squeak, skreeeek! He lay in his bed, the gears of his mind turning as they had every morning this week, trying to imagine what might be the source of this new and annoying alarm clock across the hall. A giant hamster wheel? A mysterious rusty weight-lifting machine?

JP'd missed the move-in of his new neighbour, though he knew from Zahra that she had sublet studio 7C while she was away at an ashram in India. He had not seen the new tenant.

Perhaps it had happened when he'd been out with the kids shopping or to the playground. As if conjured by his thoughts, his two toddlers waddled, rubbing their sleepy eyes, towards his bed. He glanced at the blinking red numbers on his bedside clock. 7:30 am. Thank you neighbour.

"Good morning, Sleepyheads." He opened his arms and invited them to climb in with him. Christian managed without a struggle, his four-year-old limbs plenty powerful enough to haul his sturdy frame onto the high mattress with a bounce. Fifi needed help, though. JP reached over and lifted his plump two-year-old up and above his head, lowering her to kiss her silken sleepy face and tickle her with a raspberry on her sweet-smelling baby neck. The tinkle of her giggles rewarded him, erasing any trace of his grumpy mood.

"Morning, Papa," said Christian, bouncing again. JP reached one hand over to touch his son's thigh, a silent reminder against vigorous bed-jumping.

Fifi leaned in and pressed her puckered lips against JP's bristled cheek, regarding him with her wide blue eyes. JP wondered, not for the first time, if his wife's death somehow explained why his daughter had not yet spoken a word at two-and-a-half. Christian had been talking their ears off by eighteen months, though it had been monosyllabic to begin. Or was it, as he feared, a shortcoming in his solo parenting that caused Fifi's silence.

He pulled Fifi close and squeezed her, kissing the top of her head. "I love you, Fifi," he whispered against her ear. If his silent grief after Fiona's death was in any way responsible, he would make it up to her. Christian suffered no such symptom. He already chattered about his day.

"Did you say you're going fishing today?" JP asked.

Christian tossed his head back and giggled as though JP's question were the height of absurdity. "Nooo, Papa! Car-y-um," he answered. "We're going see fish and b'luga, Papa."

"Aha, the aquarium. I see. That will be fun. I guess we need to make you a lunch, then, yes?"

The rest of the morning unfolded as it usual with Jean

Philippe dutifully providing the care and attention for his children that Fiona had once done while he ran his firm, that he now undertook in her stead without complaint. Only once he'd settled his children in bed, and a measure of housework done to keep the chaos at bay, could he begin his workday. He had a client coming by at ten. Thank God, this live-work studio made it possible. Not easy, no never that. But possible. In contrast, continuing to run his large graphic design firm would have been impossible, though he missed it as much today as the day he walked out.

On their way out to take Christian to his preschool a block away, JP glared at his neighbour's door, closed, immovable and silent as a church until the early evening encore of the curious noise. He wondered what went on in there.

Two days later, Lucy bid her morning guests good bye, then stepped out into the hall to glance both ways. The corridor jogged back and forth, with each studio entrance indented like a small porch. Many of her neighbours decorated and furnished these tiny spaces to personalize them. There were benches, artworks, plants, and signs that told her what they did. Light flooded in columns into the space, helping the plants grow, showing the weather and the changing time of day, contributing to the feeling that it was a street lined with tiny houses.

Anna paused. "Hey, Lucy? I miss you already. Why don't you join a few of us from the department for drinks this evening at the Frog and Firkin? Everyone wants to see you."

Lucy turned to answer her and noticed someone who peeked through a cracked open door across the hall in 7D. She pretended not to notice.

"I don't know, Anna. I'd love to catch up with you. But I feel…" Lucy cast a glance toward the hidden eavesdropper, hesitant to air her dirty laundry. "I don't want to put a damper on your Friday night cheer. I'd better not."

Anna shook her head and hugged Anna as she said, "You wouldn't. Ignore those creeps. They're just jealous of your famous grandfather and the fact that the department head thought your project worthy of a sabbatical."

Lucy watched Anna shrink down the long corridor and turn a corner at the far stairwell. No. They weren't jealous. Anna was okay, but she knew a few of her work colleagues thought she was nuts. She hadn't been out of grad school long enough to risk her prestigious research position on a crazy vanity project to redeem an old man's reputation. An old man who was long forgotten, and moreover, dead. It wouldn't advance her own career, either, though they'd accused her of that.

Lucy bent to poke a finger into the soil of her bamboo plant, sensing for moisture, and addressed the peeping Tom, who still watched her, or at least hesitated to close the door and draw attention to themselves. It was likely a nosy older person.

"Hello? Can I help you?"

Silence. Staring at the gap in the door, she straightened. She sensed them still there, holding their breath.

"I know you're there. Come out and introduce yourself." She turned to face the neighbour's door, smiling "I'm Lucy."

After another long, awkward silence, the door creaked opened a few inches.

Oh, hello neighbour!

CHAPTER TWO

LUCY FELL BACK A STEP, her jaw dropping to see a youthful, sexy Dr. Who standing in his doorway. Not the nosy granny she'd expected. Though he was wearing plaid flannel pyjama bottoms, from which she tore her curious gaze. He was a tall, lean, incredibly hot guy with black bedhead and sexy scruff. Her mouth went dry.

He blinked at her. His vivid blue eyes radiated kindness, and she smiled at his obvious embarrassment. She saw, in a flash, her grandfather's steady aquamarine gaze, and how it made her feel so seen and so centred. It was like that.

"Oh! H-hi." She tugged her top down.

The gorgeous man was slow to speak, but as he opened the door wider and stepped through it, his lovely toned chest rose and fell with a deep sigh, and pink tinge his bearded cheeks. His throat moved as he swallowed.

"I'm sorry. I didn't mean to spy on you." He rubbed his beard-shadowed face with the back of his hand and then raked his fingers through his messy hair, grimacing, as though checking himself in an imaginary mirror and finding his reflection lacking.

"Yes, you did. That's exactly what you meant to do." She laughed. "But it's okay. Hi, again. I'm Lucy." She put out her hand. "I'm new here."

He huffed, glanced over his shoulder, then stepped forward and took her hand, shaking it, with a flash of teeth that disappeared. "Yeah, I know. Nice to meet you Lucy. I'm, ah… Jean Philippe. JP to my friends." He spoke softly, almost a whisper.

"Hello, JP." Lucy brought a hand to cover her mouth, unable to restrain the grin of amusement that pulled at her face. His embarrassment and shyness were so endearing. And weird, because he was a super handsome hunk she would usually be too shy to talk to. She had a hard time tearing her eyes from his sculpted pecs to meet his warm blue gaze, feeling more than her own share of embarrassment for ogling him.

"Can I do something for you?"

Then he pulled himself together, shaking his head and chuckling. He tugged his shoulders back, ran his hand over his bare chest, self-conscious of her gaze on his bare skin. "I apologize. You've caught me at a disadvantage." He drew a breath. "I was spying, I admit. But only because of the mystery sound."

"Sound?"

"Yes. All week I've woken up to a mysterious, uh…" He imitated the noise, squeak, squeak, squeak, and she smiled in response to the funny face he pulled, and the crazy, curious brightness that shone in his vivid blue eyes. "I thought maybe if I peeked out before the noise at seven thirty, I'd discern its origin."

She processed that. "You set an alarm before the…"

He nodded, his dark brows lifting in apology.

"Ah. I see." She cleared her throat. "Well, that I can explain. So sorry I've been waking you. I have to get some… something to fix it, but I haven't yet."

He stood, eyes wide, waiting for the information he sought.

"Right, so–"

Just then a small face popped around the door jamb and mashed itself against his thigh, startling her. She flinched and squealed before realizing it was an adorable little boy, four or five, his full round cheeks pink and creased, his eyes still sleepy. She smiled, her chest filling like bread rising in a warm kitchen.

JP dipped his chin. "Ah, good morning Christian." He ruffled the boy's messy auburn hair, smiling at him. He took him by the shoulders and moved him like a chess pawn in front of his knees. "This is Lucy. Our new neighbour. Say hello, please."

The boy gazed up at her with cautious curiosity. "Hello, Lucy."

"Where is Fifi?"

Christian turned to look behind him where a second tiny face shone in the shadow behind them. "Ah, Fifi, darling." JP twisted, bent and straightened with a tiny dark-haired girl in an onesy covered in butterflies and bumble bees. "And this is Fifi. My daughter."

"Hello Fifi," Lucy smiled at the girl, but got only a wide-eyed blue stare and a serious cupie-doll mouth for her efforts. Oh, my God she was cute. Lucy met JP's gaze, grinning. She tilted her head. "Nice to meet you, Christian." Lucy crossed her arms in front of her. Here she was ogling this man's naked chest and handsome face when his wife was lying in bed somewhere behind that door. "I didn't realize there were families living in any of the studios," she said to the floor, then glanced along the hallway.

JP nodded. "A few, yes. Special circumstances. I'm a web designer and work from home, and it's just us so I have to live somewhere I can…" He shrugged, as though that made sense. "Work."

Just us? "Okay. Did you want to see what makes the mystery noise?"

"The squeak?" Christian said.

"Oh, so you've heard it too, have you?" Lucy said and turned to her door. "Come and see then." She led them inside, standing by the open door as JP, carrying Fifi, and Christian, tiptoed into her dim space, looking around as though entering a haunted house. Together, they gave off a lovely, warm, domestic aroma of warm skin, fresh laundry and sour milk that had her hormones swooning and fanning their faces like little groupies at a rock concert.

"What's this?" Christian said and sat on a stack of yoga blocks. "Why don't you have any chairs?" he chattered.

"Christian!"

"It's okay." Lucy laughed at his look of horror. "I teach yoga classes twice a day, early, before my students go to their workplaces, and again in the evening." The floor was still littered with yoga gear, but she stepped across the strewn blocks and blankets toward her screen. "This is the culprit. I have to move it back and forth twice each day, between yoga and my other work." She waved her arm back and forth, painting its diurnal path, like the sun across the sky.

JP squinted, tilting his head to see behind the screen,

blinking at her paper-strewn work table. Then looked at its blocky wooden feet. "So these legs squeak? That's it?" He chuckled, shaking his head. He rubbed the back of his neck with one hand, drawing Lucy's gaze to his flexing biceps and gorgeous stretching pecs and lats. Cotton fluff filled her mouth. He must work out to keep in such amazing shape. The computer-geeky types she'd dated before were skinny, enervated, like sprouts run up in a dark cupboard.

"You can't know how many fanciful explanations I've come up with this week, lying in bed imagining." He waved his arm above his head, displaying yet more pretty muscles. Lucy forced the image of him lying in bed out of her head. "Elaborate machinery. Some Steampunk inventor's lair. Or a torture chamber."

It was Lucy's turn to laugh. What an imagination! "Sorry to disappoint. Just plain old friction." The moment the words were out of her mouth she felt her face heat. Jeez. Why did the word friction conjure images of skin on skin, limbs tangling, heavy breathing. He's married, married, married. Stop it Lucy.

"You have boy hair like Papa," Christian observed, generating yet another grimace of apology from JP. She grinned. "Mama's hair's rust like mine, but really long." He pointed to his elbow. "Do you have a cat? Cats are soft but Papa says we can't have a cat. Do you have kids? There's no kids to play with here. That's why I go to school."

"Shh, Christian. Not so many questions, okay?" He gently set fingers over the little boy's mouth. "We just met Lucy."

"But I like her!" Christian shrugged and pulled away, his voice tapering off, happy enough talking to himself. He bent to stack the yoga blocks. "I like going to school because I can play with Lawrence. He's my friend. He has red hair like me. But he has spots…"

"Sorry," JP said.

"They're really cute," she said to put him at ease, trying not to laugh out loud.

JP's cheeks had bloomed with colour at his son's rambling. He set Fifi down beside her brother and walked to the screen, grabbing the edge and moving it a bit. Squeak! "I see."

"Um. Yeah, so it's awfully heavy. And I have to push it an inch at a time, from here…" she pointed. "To here. So I can, um, pull out my work table." She waved her hands, palm down, to show the space she spent her days bent over the table piled with notebooks and files, the underside stacked with file boxes.

He squatted to examine the feet, then stood. "Industrial casters would be best, eh? Silent, and much easier for you. It's incredibly heavy."

"Yes. I guess."

"Do you want a hand with it?"

"Oh, that's not–"

"My friend Mark is coming to work with me around ten, ten thirty. If you buy the casters, we can help you tip it over and screw them on the bottom."

She thought a moment. How would she do it herself? She couldn't. Ever since two burly moving men delivered the thing, she'd been struggling with it. "Thank you. If you have time, and it's not a bother?"

"No bother. I'm handy with tools. And I'm just across the hall." He smiled then, with straight white teeth set off against his dark beard, and she felt another wave of wooziness. Gosh, he was handsome.

"Your… wife… won't mind?"

His smile and his gaze dropped to the floor, and he stared at his children. "I no longer have… but she wouldn't have minded, no. I'm happy to help a neighbour." He flashed a tight smile at her. "I'll see you later."

JP and his kids returned home and resumed their morning routine. But it was no longer routine. Routine was irrevocably disrupted. Now there was Lucy. And a date… no, not a date, an appointment, for later in the morning. Only to be neighbourly. He had trouble shaking off the exchange and resuming normalcy. Or what had passed for normal this past year and a half, since Fiona's death.

And there it was, the reality check he needed. For fifteen minutes, he'd almost forgotten his dead wife in the glow and sparkle of that girl across the hall. Almost forgotten his duty, and his deathbed promises.

Meeting the sweet girl across the hall had shaken him. She was so different! A bold, brilliant breath of fresh air. But nothing so clichéd as that. She was so much more. A pixie. A fairy. A sprite. With boy-length short dark hair, large dark doe eyes–so innocent–and petite, with a slender figure. She was Tinkerbell, who'd cast an instant spell on him, blanking his mind.

He'd felt like a man again, admiring a woman, and having carnal responses, instead of a dull dutiful father and a domestic drudge.

He hadn't looked at another woman in years. Once he'd met Fiona, there had been no other women. She'd been the one for him. He'd fallen hard and loved her harder. And they'd launched their careers, married and started their family at record speed. He'd never entertained a single doubt. She was his woman, for life, til death did they part.

But a long life it was not to be, and death did indeed part them. Their blissful optimistic life together had been short lived. Christian was less than two years old when Fiona's ovarian cancer was diagnosed, simultaneous with the discovery that Fifi was on the way, already eighteen weeks grown. A dual explanation for why Fiona had been feeling so ill. And then the impossible choice. He would have chosen Fiona. Naturally he would. But she had chosen Fifi. He was just glad she'd survived until Fifi was a year old. At least she had that.

Now he had Fifi but not Fiona. He would never, ever wish his delightful little daughter away, but if he could have Fiona back? The thought tortured him.

The worst two years of his life.

And since then? No women. Nothing but… this.

JP stood at the kitchen counter, waiting for his coffee to brew while the kids wandered around the studio doing their thing, which seemed to involve pulling things out and spreading them everywhere. Toys, clothes, cups, pillows and other random objects. He'd found life more peaceful once he'd stopped trying to control all that in the moment, and just clean up in one fell swoop after the kids were in daycare and school. A few times a week at least.

Drinking his coffee, his eyes scanned the piles of project notes on his corner desk. He did his graphic and web design work at home now, alone, so the days that Fifi were with him were chaotic and scattered. Most of what he accomplished happened while she watched shows, napped, or in the evenings while both kids slept. Every second day, on Mondays, Wednesdays and Friday mornings, she went to daycare while Christian was at pre-school. Then JP cleaned, did laundry, tidied up, shopped, scheduled his client meetings, and blitzed on projects. Today was one of those days. They had to head out soon.

"Time to go, Christian. Put on your shoes."

"'Kay, Papa," he answered, looking up. Christian needed at least a half an hour warning to get ready.

JP loved his kids. And he'd vowed to be the best of fathers for them without fail. But the hours and the days rolled one into the next, leaving him numb and detached. And he got lonely for adult companionship. Today, unlike most days, he was eager to get on with it. He could look forward to something unusual. A meeting with his beautiful new neighbour. Who was nothing like his wife.

A shiver of excitement ballooned in his chest.

A momentary distraction, however. There could be no romance in this dad's life anytime soon. Not a chance.

LUCY TIDIED up the yoga gear, counted and put away her money and ate a light breakfast, but she couldn't even contemplate starting her work for the day. First, there was no point struggling with the heavy screen if JP–Jean Philippe–would be here in two hours to flip it over and... And secondly, she had to run out to the hardware store and find casters and screws. Also, because there's no way she could concentrate on Grandpa's papers in her current state of mind.

She wouldn't have minded, he'd said of his wife. He no longer had a wife, he'd said.

Was he divorced? The way he worded it though sounded as if she was... dead? If that were true, oh my. Those poor little children. That poor man. Lucy huffed and shook her hands as though she'd picked up something too hot to handle. Maybe she had.

He was beautiful and sweet, and she wasn't talking about little Christian. She stood in the middle of her studio just picturing him, so bashful and polite, so kind and lovely and... and freaking hot! She swallowed.

Lucy didn't need a distraction. She'd only just got started on her important project. Time was short, resources shorter. She couldn't afford to waste a single day if she intended to review and compile her notes and figure out how to fight Sinnehausser before it was too late.

But all she could think about was getting casters and screws and maybe picking up something from the bakery so she could offer Jean Philippe a coffee and keep him around just a little longer.

She grabbed her purse and coat and raced out the door.

LUCY HAD HURRIED FOR NOTHING, and wasted the morning, when she could have got work done. She'd bought the hardware the old guy at the store had recommended and she hoped it would work. She had made coffee and her box of pastries sat on the kitchen counter. But it was almost eleven, and he hadn't come.

Stupid girl.

So he was kind and sweet and wonderful to look at.

What was she thinking? She neither wanted nor needed a man in her life. Never mind a single dad with two little kids. She was just getting started on her career, and she'd just embarked on a near-impossible challenge that was more important to her than anything. What would she do if he asked her out? She'd have to decline, anyway. She couldn't afford the time off.

Pouting, she stared at the closed door. It was okay. He wasn't coming. He was too busy.

Knock, knock!

She jumped. Oh, crap. That was him. Dashing to the door, she calmed herself. She was way too excited. This was bad. She opened the door, almost hoping for another glimpse of his bare chest. Instead he wore faded jeans and a baseball shirt that hugged his lovely pecs, hiding but not hiding them from her view. "Hi!"

"Sorry I'm late. I… my friend couldn't stay to help. He's a client. We had to get through a meeting before he left to another appointment so…"

Oh. Oh. She shook herself alert. Just the two of them then. Alone. "Come in. That's fine. I just got back from the hardware store." She stepped aside, and he stepped in, a yellow and black plastic toolbox in one hand. The muscles and sinews on his bare forearm caught her eye. She had to stop ogling him.

"Lucy?"

"Huh?"

"Is this okay? Is now a good time to do this?"

She nodded. "Mm-hmm."

He strode to the screen. "Does this stuff come off? I have to lay it on the floor. I don't want to hurt it." He plucked at the silky sari fabric, peering at her.

She shook her head. "It's okay. I stapled it on so, don't worry about it. And the floor's clean... because of the yoga?"

"All right." He set down his tool box. "I could have used Brian's help but..."

"I can help."

He scanned her from her chin to her toes and back again, one side of his mouth quirking. "Um. No. No offence but you're too petite. Rather tackle it alone. I'd feel terrible if I dropped it on you."

Hmph. She folded her arms across her chest and stood watching while he positioned himself at the centre of the screen and stretched his arms wide, gripping it top and bottom. Then he bent his knees, squatted and lifted and angled it until it was more horizontal than vertical. His shoulders were broad and well-shaped and she watched in awe. The muscles she'd seen this morning bunched and flexed as he worked. It didn't make her feel tiny and weak, no it didn't.

"Now what?" He was in the screen's way and unable to set it down.

He looked over his shoulder, his eyes bugging. "Uh, maybe I could set it on something?"

"Yes! I'll..." She looked around. She had no chairs. She ate standing in the kitchen or sitting on the floor. There was no table. She ran to the shelves under the window and grabbed a stack of foam yoga blocks. "Will these work?"

"Yes. Anything." He grunted. "I should have planned this out better."

She ran over and set them on the floor beside him, stacking them. He shifted and twisted until he could set the edge of the frame on top of the stack.

"That's good." He stood up, panting, a sheen on his brow. "That is one heavy… what is it, anyway?"

She pulled at a loose edge of sari silk to show him. "An old chalkboard."

"Oh! Freaking slate! No wonder it's so heavy!" He laughed.

"Would you like a glass of water? Or coffee?"

"I'll get this hardware on first, okay?"

Obviously. This wasn't a social call. He was being a Good Samaritan. A helpful neighbour. A manly man. She sighed. Not boyfriend material anyway. Not that she was looking. She got the bag of hardware from the kitchen. "I hope these work. The guy at the store recommended them."

JP took the bag and peeked in. "Yeah. These'll do just fine."

He set to work, pre-drilling then screwing the metal plates attached to the casters onto the bottom of her screen's legs. "I hope it's stable once they're installed. I don't want this thing to topple over. It would crush you." He drilled and screwed a few more. "These should be far enough apart."

She nodded and smiled and watched him work, sighing. "I appreciate this so much. Thank you, Jean Philippe."

Before she knew it, he was finished. Watching his sinewy strong arms handle the tools, his intent, serious blue eyes focussed on the task, was no hardship. She could have done it all day. He put away his tools and with much effort, hefted the screen back onto its pins like an Olympian, rocking it, testing the stability now it was two inches higher off of the ground. Then he wheeled it back and forth, trying out the wheels. "Try it!"

She did. "That's amazing! It doesn't even feel heavy. I can move it easily."

"Well, it's still heavy, so don't be shoving it hard or it could get away from you. Maybe go out the window."

Shocked at the notion, she stared at the large panelled glass at the end of the large room. Nah. She frowned at him.

He flashed a teasing grin, and she swooned again at his smile. "Kidding. But it could crash into the wall. And it could tip over under force. So promise me you'll be careful, okay?" His head tilted forward.

She nodded. Please don't leave. She smiled. "Coffee?"

"I'd love one. Thanks."

She offered him a pastry, and he ate one while sipping his coffee, leaning against her kitchen counter.

She faced him, mirroring his pose, watching him eat. "Sorry I have no furniture."

"Where do you sleep?"

She waved at the floor. "On Zahra's futon. Zahra is a minimalist. And I don't need anything to tie me down. I'm here only long enough to complete my work."

"And what's that?"

"Um. It's kind of complicated. Aside from the yoga, I'm on a short break from my university job so I can do research on a personal project. And I'm on a tight deadline. So no fooling around." Oh shit. "I mean…"

He grinned. "I understand. I get little opportunity to play either, with my situation."

"I guess. So your wife…?"

His brief smile vanished. "Fiona. Ovarian cancer. A year and a half ago."

Her face tightened. "I'm so sorry," she whispered, her eyes burning.

His mouth flattened, and he nodded. "Yeah. Thanks." He rubbed the back of his neck. "But... this is my life now. I work, and I parent, and I do housework. That's pretty much it. Twenty-four seven. No time for fooling around either." He smiled. "Tell me about your special project."

CHAPTER THREE

"MY GRANDFATHER, PROFESSOR HENRY CLOUGH..."

JP studied her as she spoke. She paused, choked up, and dabbed the corners of her eyes. Grief was never so far removed from JP's world that he wasn't right there with her, tears welling in sympathy, his throat thickening.

"Sorry." She sniffled. "He died, too. And I miss him so much. It was three years ago. I was still away finishing grad school, so I wasn't able to spend the time with him that I would have liked. But he wasn't himself at the end, anyway." She met his gaze. "Alzheimer's."

He nodded, waiting for her to go on. He stared at her for the few moments it took her to gather herself. She wore one of those strappy yoga tops that bared a lot of skin–smooth pale skin–that contrasted with her short dark hair. She has a small tattoo on her exposed shoulder. He tilted his head to see it better. A flower of some sort, on the flat plane of her sharp scapula that stood proud of her lean back like a bat wing, fragile but somehow sprung with energy. He had a sudden image of her sprouting wings and taking flight. He twitched with the urge to reach out and touch it with a fingertip.

She drew a breath. "He spent his career, his whole life really, researching cognitive science and perception."

"Whoa. Heavy stuff. And you're... what? Doing the same kind of work?"

"No. My Master's is in psychology." She rocked her hand back and forth. "So I'm stretched with his research. But I'm trying to prove, and document, how his research and writings over forty years or so led to recent developments in understanding perception and pattern recognition, especially in relation to information theory in STEM field pedagogy."

"Do you understand what you just said? Because I'm not sure I do."

She laughed roughly. "Like I said, I'm out of my comfort zone too. But the idea behind my research is to find specific references and ideas in his journals, research notes and papers that lead up to end points. To connect the dots. To prove that it was what he was doing all along. And to create a kind of memoir and... tribute."

She leaned in, meeting his gaze earnestly, and hairs lifted on his skin as he drew nearer to her in response. She touched his arm with the cool tips of her fingers, nodding, and his skin tingled, his nostrils flaring at the close sweet scent of a woman. It had been too long. "See, the problem is, he lost his beautiful brain, in the end. He started to get sick about six or seven years back." Her voice broke, her large dark eyes glassy with emotion. "Before it all got pulled together and published. And now his stupid protegé–a researcher named Peter Sinnehausser–is publishing a book and taking all the credit." He smiled at the way her shoulders tightened and her chin jutted with determination, and she pulled at her fingers over and over, twisting them.

"Oh. Yes, now I understand." He dipped his chin and frowned, understanding the weight of her challenge. It was daunting. She seemed so young, fresh and innocent to be taking on such a serious academic project all on her own. He chided himself for the stupid thought, but there was something about this spritely young woman that brought out his inner caveman, with a corresponding desire to protect and possess.

"Information theory is so important now that AI and robotics are being developed. It's not as theoretical as it once was. His research findings could help map more precise measurement of perceptual expertise and… and what's the word. Um. Progression." She nodded, her hands fisting as she stared across the room.

He shrugged, wondering if she remembered that he was there, or that she was talking to a stranger. JP didn't have a clue about the research, but her determination impressed him, and it seemed important to her. So he kept nodding and vocalizing agreement. He knew this amazing, bright young woman would make sense of her grandfather's research, somehow, given enough time.

"My grandpa was the wisest, kindest and most generous of men. He was my inspiration. I absolutely adored him." She wagged her head side to side. "And I was so heartbroken that he declined while I was away at grad school when I'd promised myself I'd spend time with him before it got too bad. I never got to say goodbye and I miss him so much." She inhaled sharply through her nose, and again tears welled in her lovely dark eyes, this time spilling over.

He leaned in and gave into the desire to touch her soft arm, nodding. He wanted to wipe the tears from her cheeks, but was cognizant of his awkward position.

She sniffed. "So I can't let this happen. You know what I mean?"

"Yes. I think I do. It's important, Lucy, what you're trying to do. No matter what the outcome, it's a worthy endeavour."

She nodded, dashing away her own tears at last with the heels of her hands, meeting his gaze. "Thank you. Thank you for listening. I'm sorry, I... I get carried away sometimes. I'm determined to achieve my goal in the time I have."

"Don't worry about it. I understand. How much time do you have?"

"Just two months."

"It's not unlike..." he stopped, unsure it was appropriate.

"Unlike what?"

He tilted his head, relenting. It might ease her discomfort if he shared something too. It's just as well he was clear about his own lack of availability.

"Not unlike the promise I made to my wife, before she died." He hesitated. "Not only that. I will keep my word to her, but also I want to. To devote myself to raising my kids. Not to off-load their care." He hesitated, his voice softening. "I mean I use some daycare. I have to. But I really want to be there for them. They only get one parent, so I want it to count. I want to be the best father for them. So they can grow up knowing how much they're loved." The part he never voiced was how sick he still was about letting Fiona doing everything before, while he focussed on his career.

She nodded, gripping his hand in hers. "I get it. You're so right. I admire your commitment."

"Except mine has no deadline. I'm in it for years." He shrugged. "Forever."

Silence fell between them, each preoccupied with their own thoughts for a moment. Her obsession was admirable, because he was not looking to get in her way. I don't need anything to tie me down, she'd said the other day. He didn't have the time to help nor hinder her progress. They'd be friends and neighbours. It would be nice to have a friendly neighbour. Better than Zahra, who was eccentric and always had people over. At least for a little while.

Lucy stepped back, lacing her fingers together in front of her stomach. "I'm sorry, JP. I've done it again." She shook her head and smiled, chagrined, and warmth coiled in his chest. "Thank you so much for helping me with my partition today. I realize I couldn't have done that myself. Now I can move it with ease, and I won't be bothering you or my other neighbours anymore with my weird noises." She leaned in and pecked his cheek, then withdrew, dropping her gaze. "You're so sweet."

He touched his cheek where her soft lips had landed. It was time to go. JP stepped toward the door, conscious he'd overstayed his welcome. "Happy to help. No bother at all. And it was great meeting you Lucy. Thank you for explaining your project. I wish you well."

She followed him, stopping a few feet away, leaning against the counter. Their fleeting moment of intimacy now seemed both implausible and inappropriate, and he was eager to leave.

"I'll see you around I hope. I don't get out much but I'm sure we'll bump into each other in the hallway now and then."

He nodded. "Sure. Just knock on my door if you have any other… problems. Good-bye."

OVER THE NEXT couple of weeks, Lucy's life fell into a calm, comfortable routine, alternating between teaching her yoga classes and diligently hunching over her grandfather's notes, day in and day out without a break. She didn't see the point in taking breaks. Time was short.

On the weekends, she tidied up the studio and did her laundry, as she was doing now, in the communal laundry room on the ground floor of the building.

If she ever spent a few minutes gazing out the window wishing for her normal life, with her eight-to-four job and an actual social life, a beach vacation or a visit to a spa, she reminded herself that this was temporary. And she reminded herself why she'd chosen this path, and why it was so important.

Grandpa Henry had been her idol growing up. She'd adored him, and he'd returned the favour by doting on her. The youngest of three kids, daughter of two stressed-out, hard-working academic parents, she'd always known that everyone around her had something more important to do. Grandpa was the only one who seemed to see her. He was the only one that had time for her and made her feel special. It made all the difference.

She admired what Jean Philippe was trying to do. It would be easy, almost expected, for any man in his situation, busy as he was building his business, and supporting his family, young, active and virile, to hire someone to care for his children as he carried on as before. No-one would blame him for that. But he'd made a conscious choice to be different. To be the main caregiver for them, to give them security and continuity, while carrying the remaining load.

They'd passed in the hall only a few times, each time one or the other busy and preoccupied, unable to stop and chat. He was juggling kids and groceries, or bidding a client good bye as they left. She likewise surfaced mainly to welcome her yoga students and see them off. Like clockwork. If he'd wanted to chat, he could catch her. But he hadn't. He only smiled or waved.

Her initial reaction to him was a bit ga-ga. She still thought about that first morning, his gorgeous naked chest and pyjamas, his messy bed head and embarrassed silence. The mental picture made her weak-kneed with lust.

If she hadn't gone on and on that day, and if they both didn't have far more important things to do, that might have led to some major distractions.

She got a little weird when talking about Grandpa Henry. She sighed and continued on down the empty hall with her basket of clean laundry. Before she arrived back at her door, she heard a commotion.

"Fifiii, noooo. Don't touch that, lovey."

Sometimes there were sounds that escaped his studio, and though she tried not to eavesdrop, she had caught snippets of the general chaos that reigned inside. He seldom raised his voice, but there was often a note of exasperation. And thuds and crashes. But despite the physical chaos, he seemed to keep it all together. JP was organized, disciplined, hard-working, mature, and totally, utterly committed to his kids.

He was admirable and selfless to a fault.

Sometimes she found herself standing at her door, peering out her peephole at the empty corridor, just wondering. Did he ever come out to play?

As she came up level with his door, he suddenly burst out of it, closing it behind him and slumping back against it with his eyes closed.

She stopped and stared at him, mouth open. He was still, except for the rapid rise and fall of his chest as he panted, sucking air through clenched teeth. Then he mumbled something under his breath, like a prayer.

"Jean Philippe?" she whispered, afraid to startle him. "Are you all right?"

His eyes flew open with a gasp. He flinched and stood upright. "Oh." He exhaled and hung his head, scrubbing his already messy hair with his clawed fingers. "I will be. I had to get out before I said or did something I'd regret."

"What happened?"

With his mouth pulled tight he lifted his gaze to hers. "Fifi just deleted my entire project. A full week's work."

"Are you serious!" Her hand flew up to her mouth. What if that had happened to her notes? She'd be freaking out.

"You're a patient man." Even more to admire.

"She's getting more curious and mobile every day, so it's been a challenge to keep her away from my work computer and things." He shook his head. "The thing with toddlers is, the more taboo something is, the more they want to know about it."

"I'd have lost it, I'm sure." She laughed.

He sighed. "It's not worth losing my temper over. Nothing is as important as their safety and security and unconditional love. After all they've lost, a bit of work is nothing, is it? I won't traumatize my children because I lack self-control." He shook his head and smiled. "If my computer crashed and I lost a file... You just do it over right? Out of your control." He shrugged, "It's life. Shit happens."

"Don't you have... um, some kind of safety precautions?"

"Yes. But they're fast the little devils. I just got up to refill my coffee cup in the kitchen, and while I did that, Christian dumped an entire box of cereal on the floor. By the time I turned around, Fifi was at the computer. It was sheer random luck she deleted the file."

"I wouldn't say luck." She sent a sympathetic smile. "Can you restore it?"

He nodded. "Some, perhaps. But I got up early and made a lot of progress this morning. I'm not sure I'll get it all back."

The door behind him cracked open. "Papa?"

"I guess there's no school or day-care on weekends, hey."

He shook his head. "No."

Christian stepped out shyly. "Hi, Lucy."

"Hi, Christian." She looked up. "Do you want me to watch the kids while you go get your computer looked at?"

"Uh. Thanks, but no. I'll have to call a tech to come in. I know a guy."

"I want to, Papa. I like Lucy's house."

"No, C. We can't bother Lucy."

"Do you never leave them? For anything? Not even a

night off?" Lucy's brows pinched together as she frowned. He went on, week after week, without help? She'd never met a father so selfless and dedicated to his children.

"Not... unless I have to. I let my in-laws take them Saturday afternoons for a sleepover. It gives me a little rest. That's when I work out... play football with some friends. Then they bring them back Sunday midday."

Though that sounded like a good set up, he didn't seem happy about it. Curious, she was even more sorry for him. "Well, hey, if you get some time alone, would you like to grab dinner or something? After your football game? You need to get out once in a while, don't you?"

A loud crash came from inside.

"Shit! Gotta get back. Sorry." He turned to the door, then spun back. He dragged a hand over his beard-shadowed chin. "I'm sorry Lucy. I don't date. My life just doesn't accommodate much time for myself right now."

Her chest squeezed a little at his blunt rejection, even though it was stupid. He hardly knew her. He wouldn't leave his kids with her, or for her. And he wasn't interested in dating someone like her, too immature and unsettled. If anything, he'd be interested in a new mother for his children. She felt a little bit worthless. It reminded her of all the times her busy parents or older siblings had shunted her aside .

That's when Grandpa Henry often stepped in to suggest a game, an ice cream or a Dr. Who episode to sooth her. Grandpa never made her feel unwanted or second rate.

Well, she'd go spend more time with Grandpa Henry right now. He needed her, and she'd committed to be there for him.

She nodded across her laundry basket. "Right. Okay. Well, good luck with your file then."

He turned to the door and then back again. "Thank you, Lucy."

"For?"

"The perspective." He smiled, his eyes creasing with relaxed humour and he disappeared inside. The drama of his daily life was reduced to mumbled voices, muffled noises and the occasional bump.

CHAPTER FOUR

Lucy had spent what felt like a thousand hours bent over Grandpa Henry's notebooks through the weekend. She straightened and stretched her back, rotating her shoulders to loosen the tight muscles. She was making good progress and finding a thread of logic to tie it all together. It was still impossible to say whether she understood his work well enough to argue that Peter Sinnehauser had stolen his ideas. But she was determined to expose Grandpa's work so he would get credit for it.

In the middle of the day on Sunday, muffled knocking from the corridor outside her door interrupted her focus. She glanced up and, as she often did, ignored it and carried on. But the knocking repeated joining muted voices that escalated in volume, sounding irritated. Something going on out there.

She peeped through the viewer in her door. Two people stood at JP's door. Lucy stepped out. The man, who was short, pockmarked with receding faded orange hair, carried a backpack, a small suitcase and Christian, who was kicking to be free.

"Lemme go!"

"Settle down, Christian, lad." The man grumbled with a slight Scots burr and set Christian on the floor. "Stay put."

"Knock again, Angus. He must be here. He knows what time we come. There's no excuse." The woman, who held Fifi, a diaper bag, and a large purse, was oblivious to her presence.

The man turned toward her, his mouth pulling into a wide flat line, as though he were unaccustomed to smiling and it hurt a little. "Oh, hello. Have you seen John Philip?" He pronounced it the English way instead of the French way that JP said it. Which was odd considering they had his children. Evidently, these were Fiona's parents, his in-laws. You'd think they'd know how to pronounce their son-in-law's name.

The woman turned her shrewd eyes onto Lucy and snapped, "Don't be ridiculous, Angus, do you think his neighbours have nothing better to do but to keep tabs on him. Call him." She nudged her chin toward him, as if his hands were less full than her own. She was tall, big-boned, bossy and bitter, and reminded Lucy of her mother's sister, the average one who spent her life clawing her way out from the shadows cast by her over-achieving siblings. "Call him and ask him why he's not here."

"Hi, Lucy," said Christian.

"Hi, Christian. I'm sure he's in the bathroom, or the laundry room," Lucy said. "JP would never forget."

"Oh, is that right?" said the woman with a pinched face, as though she'd decided long ago that nothing would ever please her. "And I suppose you know. Who are you? I've never seen you here before."

Lucy shrank back, astounded at her rudeness, wondering if it were her husband, or life in general that had disappointed her so. "I'm his neighbour." Obviously. "I only meant—"

"Papa!"

"Sorry. Sorry. Sorry." JP dashed towards them down the hall, balancing several bags of groceries in his arms. "So sorry I'm late, Maeve. I just grabbed some groceries on my way home. Sorry to make you wait. Here, here. Let me open the door for you."

Why was he being so deferential? And why were they being so nasty? Lucy stepped forward to help him with his bags, since his in-laws made no move to do so. JP smiled, chagrined, at getting caught being less than perfect. He pulled out his keys and unlocked the door standing aside so they could enter with the kids. Carrying the groceries in, he came back for the bags they had left strewn all over the hallway floor.

She could see through the open door. JP kissed and hugged his kids one at a time, as though he hadn't seen them in a month. They squealed and kissed him in return, Christian chattering away about everything they had done since they saw him last, his voice rising in volume.

They had forgotten to close the door. The couple stood in the middle of JP's studio chastising him in lowered voices, two against one. She felt embarrassed for him, and angry at these horrible people. Her stomach dropped in a too familiar sensation. It was a feeling she had felt a million times, whenever she was being scolded by her parents for being in the way, or for doing something wrong. She couldn't bear scolding in that condescending way. It riled her and made her want to pick a fight. But it was none of her business. Lucy tiptoed forward to pull the door closed so they would have privacy but just as she grabbed the handle, they stepped towards her, bustling their way back out, shuttling her aside.

"All right then."

"I don't know what to think, John Philip. You want us to believe that you are caring for these children properly all by yourself. But you grab the first opportunity to forget about them."

"I didn't forget, Maeve. I was just a little late."

"This isn't the first time," said the man, Angus. "It's a miracle the ministry hasn't come investigating."

What?

"Well, what do you expect, Angus," said the woman. "Before our Fiona passed away, he didn't lift a finger. Our dear girl did everything. I don't think I ever saw him in the kitchen, or bring groceries home. God only knows what kind of junk is in those bags. You can't expect a man to run a household."

"Hey," Lucy said. "That's not fair. You're not here every day. You don't see what he does."

Jean Philippe leaned against the door jamb, his shoulders slumping. He looked up at her, his face tense. "Lucy, don't. Please."

He sounded so tired. Lucy looked up, cross that these people who should be so appreciative of the dedication and loving care this man gave their grandchildren, could speak so harshly to him. And so unjustly. She was indignant. "But, it's not right!"

JP said, "It's all right. Let it go, please." He looked so

dejected and sad, she felt tears of sympathy flood her mouth with salt, and burn the back of her eyes. What was wrong with him? Why would he let them talk to him this way?

"I don't understand."

"Let's go, Angus. This girl is obviously some bit of fluff that's been distracting JP from his responsibilities." She jabbed a pointed finger toward Lucy. "You mind your own business, Missy. Fooling around with our son-in-law doesn't give you the right to express an opinion about the care of our grandchildren." She turned back to JP. "You'd better not be leaving these children unattended while you mess around across the hall, Mister. We'll take them away from you so fast your head will spin. I knew we couldn't trust you from the start." She pulled a tissue from her purse and to dabbed her eyes. "And to think, our poor dear Fiona gave up her life for these children. How can you be so ungrateful? I wish it was you that had died!" She sobbed and her husband wrapped his arm around her shoulders and patted her on the back.

"There, there, Maeve. There's no point getting upset. It is what it is. He's their father. And at least we're here to make sure the children come to no harm."

They turned and plodded down the corridor.

"Are you kidding me right now? How dare you speak about Jean Philippe that way." Lucy stepped into the corridor with her hands on hips. She spat, "You... people!"

"Let it go, Lucy." His voice resigned but firm, JP stepped up behind her and took her by the shoulders, steering her into his studio and closing the door. "They're gone. Forget about it."

She spun to face him, confused. "What the hell, JP? I've

never seen anything like that outside of a Dickens novel! Do you tolerate that every week?"

"Can you calm down already? They're gone. Let's try to lighten the mood around here, okay?" One corner of his mouth twitched up, as though he thought she was funny. Funny!

She stood in the middle of his studio, still too flustered to know what she was seeing. He strode to the coffee table and picked up a remote, turning on a kids' show on the TV.

"Play the penguin show, Papa," said Christian.

JP clicked. Cute little penguins shuffled across the screen, talking in a cheerful tone. Christian plopped down onto the floor, absorbed. Bending to see that the kids were content, he kissed their heads. He whisked all the bags into another room.

"You have a separate bedroom?" She was slow to process all the new information. All this domesticity. So contrary to the sexy macho man with a toolbox that had helped her out.

"Yeah. My unit's bigger than yours." He took all the grocery bags to his kitchen and put them away, gliding back and forth, at ease in his kitchen.

"Are you going to explain?"

He sighed. "I need a drink first." He got down two stemless wine goblets and poured red wine into one. "Want one?"

"Sure. I guess. Thanks."

He poured a second glass, came toward her and handed her one. A frisson of energy zinged through her from the mere touch of their fingers, and their eyes met. He jerked his gaze away, then he shrugged and took a big gulp. "Come and sit down." He moved to the big soft beat up sectional and waited for her. They sat, and she took a sip of wine, letting her gaze drift around the room, soaking in details about JP.

Aside from the family clutter, there was a large work-station opposite. A large wall unit held a jumbled assortment of books, bins, DVDs and framed photographs. A pretty redhead appeared in several pictures, with babies, JP or alone. Fiona, she presumed, loomed large in this household.

"They aren't terrible people. Just sad." He drank again, sliding a glance over to the kids, who stared at the screen, entranced. "It hasn't been that long. They're still hurting a lot."

This man's patience and kindness was limitless. "Yeah, but–"

He shook his head. "I know. I lost my wife. The love of my life. But they–" He looked over at Fifi, flipping through a hard board book on the rug, strangling a soft limp rabbit that draped over her pudgy little arm and sucking on her thumb. "They lost their only child. I can't even imagine their pain."

Lucy's throat closed up. Tears flooded her eyes in an instant. She glanced at Jean Philippe warily. His eyes were glassy too. "So you just consent to be their punching bag?"

FIFI STOOD up and waddled over to the sofa, then crawled up into JP's lap. He knew that after only one night away from him, she missed him. She was always clingy when she returned from Maeve and Angus's.

She snuggled into the crook of his arm and stuck her

thumb in her mouth, dragging her rabbit up to her chin. He bent his head to kiss her soft round forehead. Her eyes drifted closed, and he continued to soothe her by caressing her downy dark hair.

He shrugged, the familiar squeeze of guilt twisting in his stomach. "What am I supposed to do? Argue with them? What's the point? They love the kids, and they help me out every week." Besides, this was his lot, what he'd signed up for. When Fiona had made her choice, she'd also elicited a promise from him to support her. He'd lost her, but he'd follow through. No matter what. Even though her parents somehow blamed him for Fiona's decision, as though he would have willingly given up his love.

Lucy sighed, shaking her head. "Where are your folks?"

"Quebec." He stretched his head from side to side, feeling his muscles tightening up from his afternoon of touch football with the guys yesterday. And a hangover from his weekly indulgence. He slumped back against the sofa, stretching his stiff arms and arching his back, and quirked a half smile at her.

Her eyes widened, darting across his chest and away again. His dick jumped at the attention and he crossed one foot over the other knee. It was rare for him to get up close to a beautiful woman these days, and his stomach did a little flip. She was so pretty, she took his breath away. His fingers tingled with the urge to touch her soft, feminine shapes.

"Thanks for standing up for me, though. I appreciate it. It took some sting out of it today."

"You're welcome." She pouted.

"You're a little scrapper, aren't you? I didn't know that about you."

"There are many of things you don't know about me." She twisted her mouth and gave him the side eye, smiling a little, and lifted one shoulder. "I don't like to see injustice."

"What do you like?"

"What do you mean?"

He shrugged. "Favourite colour. Favourite food. Favourite TV show. Tell me something." First date stuff. Though this was definitely not a first date.

"Turquoise."

"Turquoise? That's unusual."

She chuckled. "The Caribbean sea? The stone jewelry. My grandfather's eyes."

What? "He had turquoise eyes?"

She nodded. "All my favourite things are connected to Grandpa Henry. He was my favourite person in the whole world. He was my hero."

Huh. He knew she was committed to her grandfather's project, but she really seemed to be fixated on the old man. "What else?"

"I have this little painting of the sea that used to belong to Grandpa. He picked it up on his travels somewhere in the Mediterranean."

JP liked they way her big brown eyes floated up to the ceiling when she talked, as though she was seeing pictures. The corners of her pretty lips turned up. So sweet. "And?"

"Grilled cheese sandwiches. Dr. Who."

His jaw fell open. "No! You're kidding me."

She jiggled her head. "Nope."

"Well, have I got a surprise for you, my scrappy little neighbour. I'm making grilled cheese sandwiches for dinner."

"Yay!" shouted Christian. "Grilled cheese sammiches is my fav'rite, too," he said from the living room floor.

"Doesn't miss a thing, that one."

She grinned.

"After my kiddies are in bed, in about an hour, you and I are going to watch an episode of Dr. Who together. Those are some of my favourite things, too. And I need your company tonight." He stood up and moved to the kitchen.

"I can't refuse an offer like that."

"Papa. I want 'mato soup, too," said Christian, following him into the kitchen.

"Alright, C." He served it in mugs, because that was their thing with fishy crackers swimming on top.

They sat around his small round table, Fifi in her high chair. It was more crowded than usual, but nice. Full. He smiled at Lucy, watching her eat her sandwich, mesmerized by her tongue darting out to capture strands of melted cheddar.

He was distracted by Fifi, who still needed quite a bit of help and supervision eating, and made a terrible mess, but they enjoyed their delicious gooey cheddar cheese sandwiches and soup.

"Papa. Did you 'member to tell Gran'ma that I hate chicken?"

"I did."

"Welp. Gran'ma made us eat it a-gain." Christian sighed and took another bite of his sandwich. "I threw up a little."

"Oh." JP pulled a face at Lucy over Christian's bent head and then smiled as she barely held back her grin. "Sorry buddy."

Christian gazed longingly at Lucy. "Can I stay up and watch Dr. Who with Lucy?"

Lucy's eyes popped.

"Not tonight, C. You've got school tomorrow."

He seemed to ponder that, then sighed dramatically. "School's boring."

"I thought you liked school, because of your friend Lawrence," said Lucy. "You must be very smart, Christian."

She met JP's gaze, and he mouthed pre-school, impressed that she'd remembered a random detail that came out of Christian's mouth days ago.

"I am, a'tually. Papa says so."

"Well your Papa is smart, too. So he must be right."

JP smiled his gratitude.

"What's your favourite thing to do at school?" she asked.

"Drawing pictures. Like Papa. I'm an artist, too."

While Christian pretty much dominated the dinner table conversation with his constant chatter about school, their visit to grandma and grandpa's and other random facts, Fifi made not a peep. She diligently macerated, staring at Lucy without blinking with wide wondering blue eyes. Careful, JP. It wouldn't take much for the kids to get attached to someone as sweet and warm as Lucy. His stomach pinched, suddenly stealing his appetite.

"Fifi doesn't talk?" Lucy murmured under her breath.

JP shook his head, eyes cast down. "I'm not too worried, yet," he lied. "It's probably because Christian doesn't give her much space to try. He never stops."

"That's certainly true," she laughed.

Lucy offered to wash the dishes while JP got the children ready for bed, despite his insisting she do nothing of the sort, and relax on the sofa. She had barely begun, and he was back.

"That's it? No long, drawn out bedtime rituals?"

He shook his head, no. He smirked.

"Huh. I might want to know your secret someday. Could come in handy."

"It's no big secret. They co-sleep on a cot in my room, or with me, so they self sooth."

She flicked some soap foam at him, perched her hands on her hips. "Who's your favourite Who?"

He grinned and mirrored her posture, facing her with a dip of his chin. "Easy. Matt Smith. Who's yours?"

"Tennant, of course." She made a funny face, as though the answer was obvious.

He had the urge to wrap his arms around her and squeeze, but shook it off. "You're so conservative," he teased. "I look a bit like Tennant, don't you think?" He struck a pose.

"Not in the least." She rolled her eyes. "He's got bro-own eyes." She stretched out the word as though brown were the most beautiful colour in the universe. Gazing into her huge dark orbs, he thought maybe it was.

"Pish. Details. What about the hair?" He raked his hand through, making it stand up.

She gave him the side eye. "You've got a point there."

They finished the dishes, and he pulled out his extensive collection of Dr. Who DVD's for her to choose from.

"You really are a fan. You didn't just say it to impress me."

"Why would I do that?" He mugged confusion, straight-faced and blinking, and she laughed, tossing a cushion at him. He caught it and set it aside slowly, marvelling at the light, breathless sensation that fizzed through his chest, all the way out to his tingling fingertips. His cheeks pulled taut with the smile he couldn't seem to put away. He'd almost tossed the cushion back, feeling playful enough to start a pillow fight. When did he last feel this sense of fun, of excitement, or of attraction? Not for a very long time. She made him feel human again. Watching her reaction, he couldn't stop himself from stretching his arm across the back of the sofa, gesturing with his other hand for her to get closer.

"What?"

"Come. Snuggle up."

"I–I hardly–know you. How–"

"Shh." He shook off her protests, snickering and whispering, "Just do it. This is how you watch TV. Has to be." He squinted at the remote, pretending to find the buttons to push, ignoring the cautionary voices that murmured in the back of his mind. What are you doing, JP? You're not allowed to flirt, JP. Think of Fiona, JP, and the children. You're being selfish, JP. Just for the moment, he pushed the nagging chorus away.

Lucy relented, and now sat primly beside him, tucking one foot under her butt, leaning into his shoulder just a little, sending a wave of satisfying warmth through his skin, knocking at the door of his bruised heart. He tugged on her knee to pull her closer, wrapped his arm around her narrow shoulders and looked down into her big beautiful doe eyes. He revelled in the sensation of her small delicate bones and silky smooth skin. She reminded him of a fairy or a sprite. She smelled delicious, clean and feminine and something so fresh, his senses stood up and shouted, Yeeessss! The blood rushed from his overheated head to his dick in a flash. He couldn't fight it. He didn't want to. He tugged a throw over their laps to hide the swelling under his fly.

"Lucy."

She met his gaze, wide-eyed, her pulse fluttering on her neck like a delicate leaf in a breeze, her fine nose flaring with her quivering breath. He felt his control slipping.

"I thought you didn't date," she whispered, leaning a little closer.

He made a little involuntary noise in the back of his throat. It felt almost like a whimper. "This isn't a date." She was, this was, the first time he'd felt true desire for a woman since Fiona. Sure he looked at women. A man never stopped looking. But he'd never considered touching one in a very, very, very long time. Now, it was all he could think about.

He dipped his head, keeping his gaze locked on hers, and feathered their lips together in a butterfly kiss. It was heavenly. Sensation shot through him like a lightning bolt. He waited.

Lucy's chin came up with a little jerk, and he felt it as a spasm of desire, and consent, that sent a shock-wave through his own nervous system, kicking his desire up a notch. She gripped his shirt. His pulse pounding, he went in deeper, savouring her soft full lips, gliding his lips along, darting the tip of his tongue out to steal a taste of the corner of her mouth. Her mouth opened just a little on a sigh, and he ventured in, his tongue sweeping her depths as her hand slid up his chest and curled around his neck. Their mouths locked together like Lego.

Their breath mingled in a sigh.

It's okay. This wasn't a date.

CHAPTER FIVE

NOTHING CHANGED. Contrary to her expectations, that evening with JP didn't launch an all-out romantic seduction, as it would have with any of the guys at college.

She reflected on their evening together and was a little embarrassed that they'd behaved like a sex-starved teenagers. But it relieved her that JP had played it down. It was for the best.

On Monday, after morning yoga class, Anna hung around after everyone else had left. She lingered in the hallway.

Lucy lifted her brows in a question. She had something she wanted to talk about. "Aren't you due at work?"

She shook her head. "Are you okay?"

"Me? I thought you had a… something."

"Yeah." Anna peered at her. "That was a weird class. You seem salty. Is your research going okay? Is it getting you down or… " She shrugged, "are you getting tired?"

A wave of hot embarrassment shimmered through her and Lucy blinked. "Nope."

"Well what's—"

JP's door opening interrupted them, and he stepped out of his studio with a garbage bag in his hand. She tried to ignore how sexy he was in his typical working-from-home clothes—his old long-sleeve T-shirt contoured over his muscled chest and biceps, his torn, faded jeans riding so sexy low on his lean hips. His feet were bare, and the sight of them had her temperature rising and bees buzzing in her head with the overpowering intimacy of his soft vulnerable skin stretched over lean bones. She remembered what those muscles felt like under her hands. Her face flamed with heat, her breath stalling in her throat like wadded wool.

Noticing them, he faltered, raked a hand through his messy morning hair. "Oh. Hi." He glanced at her, at Anna and his gaze locked on Lucy, running up and down her body, inhaling and exhaling on a long sigh.

Last night, they'd kissed and groped and tumbled around on his sofa for a rather long time. They actually did play an episode of Dr. Who, but he kept pausing it when the tension and desire to touch became too much. It was amazing and delicious and the liquid heat his kisses inspired still careened around her nervous system like a pinball machine, settling into a hot pool below her belly. Clack, clack, whirr, ding, ding, ding! He was so sexy.

Her breath faltered, her heart kicking against her ribcage. "Hi."

"Hi." His voice dropped low, and he swallowed, glanced up and down the hall, back to her. "Um…" He moved his mouth but no more words came out. He nodded sharply, ran his hand over his beard-shadowed chin, flashed an awkward one-sided smile and carried on down the corridor with his bag of garbage.

His lithe body strode away, his long legs, muscled back, and his tight ass in those soft old jeans entrancing in their elegance. Her limbs went all soft and warm. She may have sighed. Lucy remembered the scratch of his beard on her neck and shuddered. She still had the abraded skin in sensitive places to attest to their passionate make-out session.

"I'm coming in. Spill the tea."

"Uuuhhm. Okay?" She followed Anna back into her studio and put the kettle on.

A few minutes later, they sat cross-legged in the wide window seat on piles of blankets with mugs of hot coffee in their hands.

"What. The. Fuck. Lucy? What was that?"

Her face stretched in a wide shit-eating grin. "Nothing?"

"That was not nothing. C'mon. Spill."

"I... I... after his... we... um... I stayed for dinner and... we... uh... watched Dr. Who, and..." She lifted her shoulders to her ears and twisted her mouth to one side. How could she explain?

"How long has this been going on?"

Lucy shook her head slowly. "Nothing's going on. We're not... Nothing."

Anna sat with her mouth ajar, staring at Lucy. "He's so freaking hot. The way you were undressing each other with your eyes, hoo! That's not nothing. I'm not a total idiot. What happened?"

Lucy licked her dry lips and shook her head again.

Where should she start? Her voice came out tentative and squeaky. "We kissed? A bit? Last night."

"When did you meet him?" Anna leaned forward and yanked down the neckline of Lucy's stretchy yoga top. She'd intentionally chosen to wear a high-necked style today. "Whoah. You kissed a little. Uh-huh."

Lucy pulled her shirt back up, self-conscious, blushing again at the memory of JP's hot mouth on her skin.

Anna eyeballed her with a pinched cynical face. "So how long have you been dating?"

"Oh, we're definitely not dating."

"You skipped over dating and started sleeping together?"

"Nooooo." Lucy played a few notes on her lips with the tips of three fingers. "We're not doing that, either."

"So, somewhere in between?"

"We met. And talked a little. And we…" she gestured to the door, waving her hand in circles. "We see each other, sometimes. Sort of."

"Tell me about him!"

So Lucy did. She surprised herself with how much she had learned about JP.

"Jean Philippe. Wow, such a sexy name. Is he really French?"

"From Quebec, I suppose. But he has no accent or anything. He said his parents live there."

"What don't you know about him?"

Lucy pondered. "Mmm. Lots of things."

"Like?"

"I don't know much about his work? Except that he's creative and tech savvy. Or who his clients are… except for Brian, of course."

Anna carefully set down her coffee mug and threw herself backwards with a theatrical flourish of her arm into the air above her head. "Oh. My. God!"

"It's only a neighbour thing," Lucy tried to explain. "One tends to learn things by accident. It's not like we've had all these intimate conversations. Well, not too many."

Anna laughed and laughed. "Honey, this looks to me like a real thing. The L-word. The OTP."

"WTF are you trying to say?"

"One true pairing, girl. What are you waiting for? That dude so obviously needs a woman in his life, and he so obviously wants you. Jump on that pony and ride it to the finish line, girl."

"Oh, ew. You're so crass, Anna."

"What else could you want?"

"Oh, um. A career, maybe?" She bugged her eyes at Anna. "I've barely got started."

"You can do both, can't you? Do you realize how hard it is to find a nice, honest, hot, available man like JP? You can't pass this up."

"I'm not ready to assume the role of the mom to some dead woman's children."

Anna said, "But someday? You want all that–" she made air quotes "–too, don't you?"

Lucy shrugged. "Yeah. I suppose, eventually."

"Well, if you ask me, Mr. Delicious is perfect. If you want to have your own kid, you can pop one out in a year or two and tack it onto the squad. They'd be really close in age and grow up together. It's perfect."

"That sounds far too pragmatic and mercenary to fit my idea of happily ever after."

"The critical thing about those happily ever after

fantasies is the partnership. Finding the perfect guy. After that, life throws you curve balls and you dodge them. It's always messy. It's so much easier if you started with a guy you really, really like. You do everything else as a team."

Lucy stared at Anna. She nodded and rattled her head side to side, thinking hard about what she was saying. . "This isn't on my to-do list this year."

"It's not an either-or thing, Lucy," Anna said. "I'm older than you, and let me tell you, good guys are hard to find. I've got my career, but also been dating for ten years, believing Mr. Right is just around the corner. It's not as easy as that. There's no prince coming to sweep you off your feet... unless it's him." She gestured with her thumb towards the door. "It's been one long string of losers and relationships that didn't work out. Finding your match is really hard. The good ones get snapped up in college–like your neighbour there."

Lucy shrugged. "We give each other a lot of space. We're both really busy. It hasn't been all that long since his wife died. And he's totally committed to the kids. He's even said outright that he doesn't date."

"What do you call last night?"

"Not a date."

Anna huffed. "Create your own opportunities. There's no reason you can't carry on with your project and still let things develop with him. You can't work twenty-four hours a day. Don't put up any walls. Hear what I'm saying? Let things unfold naturally if they're meant to. Worst-case scenario, you get a lovely hookup with a handsome daddy while you're staying in Zahra's place and it ends."

Lucy shook her head. What Anna was saying made some sense. But she didn't want to corner JP or force him into something he wasn't interested in. Though, he was sure interested in her last night. She supposed he needed to release some sexual tension. Poor thing. But that didn't mean he wanted to get serious about another woman so soon after his wife died.

"Why are you so reluctant? Did you get your heart broke or something?"

"No. That's not it."

"You've dated though, haven't you? You're a beautiful girl, intelligent, fun. Guys must have asked you out."

"Oh, sure. Loads. But..."

"What?"

"Well, when I was younger, like, a teenager, and liked a boy... Grandpa Henry always was excited for me, like it was the best thing ever. And he always insisted on meeting them right away." She paused, remembering a sequence of weird dates in high school, frowning.

"And?"

"Things always fizzled. Nobody ever made the cut. I never got many second or third dates. And so I didn't have real boyfriends either."

"What do you mean, made the cut?"

Lucy sighed. "Grandpa always had a sit-down and chat with guys I was going out with. He'd... He'd ask them questions. And after we'd gone out, he'd ask me questions. Somehow, the guys disappeared, or I ended up losing interest in them."

"Why? And where the heck were your parents?"

"They were always working, so it was me and grandpa alone." She smiled, a fog of remembered fondness warming her inside. "Anyway. Either Grandpa found something to criticize about the boys, subtly, or I did it myself. There'd be some things I liked about a guy, but something else would pop up. He wouldn't have a good sense of humour, or he wouldn't be ambitious. Or he'd be dishonest, or selfish. I'd always be disappointed."

"For goodness' sake, we're talking about teenagers and college students, aren't we? Did you and your grandpa expect every young guy you met to have it all figured out? They take awhile, hey."

Lucy made a face. "No, not that. It was more about character, I guess."

"So no guy you've ever dated measured up to Grandpa's standards?"

Lucy sighed. "It was more like… nobody ever measured up compared to Grandpa himself. I loved and admired him so much, it made other guys seem kind of irritating and pathetic in comparison. They all seemed like a waste of my time."

"Possibly it was a trick. Could be your grandfather wanted to make sure you focussed on your studies instead of getting distracted like a typical teenage girl."

Lucy shook her head and stretched her legs, re-crossing them the other way. "I don't think so. He might have been over-protective. He wanted who ever I spent time with to deserve of his little princess."

"Hm. So how does 7D score on Grandpa's checklist?"

"Grandpa Henry was an amazing man. Smarter than anyone I ever met. So caring and funny. Talented in other ways, too. He was a collector of art, a connoisseur of music," she paused, remembering, "he travelled and read. And it's not like he was some old stuffed-shirt. He was fun, too. Stylish and sophisticated. We did things together. Cooked and went to art galleries and geeked over Dr.

Who. When I was with him, I knew I was somebody important."

"You didn't answer my question," Anna sang. "I didn't ask you about your grandpa. What about sex?"

Lucy's eyes bugged. "What about it?"

"Well did you get any action despite every guy you've ever met being super irritating and inadequate. Did any of them get through the grandpa chastity belt?"

Lucy shrugged, "Yeah, well, there's that. I made sure I got a taste. In college. But same thing. Nothing lasting. And I won't go around hooking up with new guys every week for sex. Yuk."

"Some girls do. You're not getting any younger."

"I'm only twenty-six."

"Hey, I'm not throwing shade. You're savage. You should be as thirsty as this girl is."

Lucy stared at Anna. She couldn't even imagine. Was she so caught up in her work she was missing out on the carefree fun of being young?

"How about that neighbour, huh?"

Lucy laughed at her friend's persistence. "He doesn't even hook up. He doesn't want–"

"The way he looked at you right now? He wants something. I would bet my Fluevogs on it." Anna's eyes widened, and she grinned like a lunatic.

"He's better than that."

"Better, as in, list-burning better?"

Lucy considered JP. He was smart, creative, funny, caring, playful, ambitious, honest. It was an impressive list of attributes. And she never knew anyone so loyal. Extremely loyal. So... not a waste of her time. But not available, either. But neither was she.

CHAPTER SIX

JEAN PHILIPPE VACILLATED. He obsessed over Lucy, reliving their incredible evening moment by moment. He enjoyed her so much, every cell in his body strained to be near her, get more of her. The physical was pretty freaking incredible after years of solitude and celibacy. More than that, being with her made him joyful. Fizzy. Energized. She was smart, fun, warm, passionate. Years ago, he'd be all over that, doing anything to make more time with her as soon as possible. JP had never been shy with girls, or inhibited when he liked someone.

Now, though, he questioned his desire and his motives. He wanted Lucy for himself, but how would that affect his kids? Christian and Fifi were his priority. He loved them. His life now was for them.

How did Lucy fit into that?

She didn't.

He realized two things– watching the way his kids looked at Lucy, gravitated so to her warmth, his kids need a woman in their lives. Someone warmer and kinder than

Maeve. Was he ready to think about that, never mind act on it? How could he ask any woman he'd just met to step into his messy complicated life? To mother children that weren't her own? He couldn't. It wasn't fair.

Even if she wanted a family, it was too risky. By the time they sorted out the relationship stuff, it would be too difficult to extricate them from the kids. They couldn't deal with that kind of disappointment and loss. Again.

Anyway, Lucy was young. She wanted to work on her career and wasn't ready for a family, as far as he could tell. How could that work? He wanted to support her career and her special project. It meant a lot to her. Even though he had the family thing under control. They'd kind of found their groove. He wouldn't expect anything from her.

But everything would change, even so.

His life was complicated, too. He needed companionship. He wanted joy and not just drudgery. Raising kids was hard work. With Fiona it had been challenging but fun when they were together. Alone, sometimes the soul-crushing loneliness caused him to lose perspective.

Fifi had been teething, low fevers disrupting bedtime off and on for weeks. Christian came home from pre-school with some new challenge or attitude shift every week. Some new problem for him to solve, or decision to make that seemed to have a significant bearing on his children's upbringing and welfare.

He carried every decision and every worry on his shoulders alone. He liked Lucy a lot. But he couldn't put his kids well-being and happiness at risk.

No obvious solution presented itself to his spinning mind.

He stared at the portrait of Fiona that sat in a place of honour on the wall unit shelves, the weight of responsibility settling heavier on his back, deflating his momentary euphoria.

He sent off a quick text to his mother, updating her about Fifi's teething woes, and asking a question or two.

His phone rang.

"*Mon Ange!*"

His mother, never more than a moment away when he needed her. Thank the stars and Steve Jobs for modern technology, because even though she was on the other end of the country, his Mama was always available to help him problem solve, and sooth his worries.

"*Allo, Maman, ça va?*"

"Fine, fine. You sound so tired, love. I can hear it in your voice."

"Mhm. I'm okay. Just feeling the overwhelm today."

"What's up?"

"Nothing much." He wouldn't mention Lucy. Maman's hopes would soar in a way he didn't need. "Just worried about Fif."

"It sounds normal, *cher*. Just make sure you give her soft things to chew. And cold things, too, are soothing. Do you still have one of those gel thingies?"

"*Oui.* She's not much interested in it. And not sleeping well."

"Just monitor her temperature. Some children's acetaminophen. That's all you can do, *mon chou.*"

A beat of silence passed.

"What else, *mon Ange?*"

He grunted, his resolved crumbling. "I have a new... neighbour."

"Oh?" That one syllable, stretched out on a scale from do to la, told him she'd interpolated and was intrigued. He smiled, knowing she wouldn't press him.

"Mhm. Her name's Lucy. I–I'll tell you about her another time."

Hearing her voice always comforted him, if only for a moment.

But he still wanted Lucy. He wanted somehow to include her in his life, but letting her too far in seemed risky. What did he want? A friend, a lover, or a partner to share his family life? Fiona was all three. He wanted Fiona back. But he couldn't have that.

And to make it all worse, he was getting way, way ahead of himself, and them. They'd spent one morning, and one fun, relaxing, and yes, stimulating evening together. And he wanted to turn it into a grand love affair in an instant. How desperate was that?

He wanted to go forward without risk. Which, he knew, was foolish.

But still. Maybe risk was something he could manage. It was best if he kept them separate. Simpler. Safer. Smarter.

JP wouldn't leave his kids. He would never get a babysitter or anything to go out on a proper date. But couldn't he get to know his neighbour a little better while the opportunity presented itself?

They could still be friends. He enjoyed her company so much. Maybe they could hang out. He could make sure those opportunities arose.

Hmm.

He could help her. Jean Philippe sat down at his computer and researched her grandfather, reading a little about the man and his career. Then he opened his software and fiddled around with design ideas. Before he knew it, the morning was gone and he hadn't done any of his own work. Instead, he had the beginning of a plan.

He got up to make lunch. Then he picked up a pen and a piece of paper and scribbled a quick note:

I CAN'T STOP THINKING *about you...*

LUCY DIDN'T SEE JP for the rest of Monday or on Tuesday. She knew he had his hands full with Fifi but she was almost afraid to venture out of her studio. While she worked hard, her thoughts drifted back to all the things that Anna had said. JP was definitely not a waste of her time.

At noon on Wednesday someone knocked at her door. When she got up to check no one stood outside. She noticed a piece of paper on the floor at her feet. She picked it up.

I CAN'T STOP THINKING *about you. I'm*
    alone today but I can't concentrate
    on my work. I want to see you.
    Come for lunch?

ADRENALINE RUSHED through her body in a tidal wave. She hugged herself and jumped up and down three times. "Oh my God. Oh my God."

It's nothing. Her excitement was unfounded. Lucy ran to her bathroom and looked in the mirror. Dirty hair and ratty yoga gear looked back. Ugh. Whatever JP wanted, he wouldn't want what she saw in the mirror. She hopped in the shower and washed her hair, then threw on her favourite Lululemon pants with a soft peach cover-up that said, Pah, this is how fresh and sexy I look every morning! She didn't anticipate anything.

She really wasn't. Seeing him would be nice, though.

She dried her hair and ran her fingers through it with gel in a way that said she'd been working, not primping. Pinching her cheeks she put on a dash of lip gloss. Her heart raced and her breath stuttered. Her hand shook as she added a few swipes of mascara.

What if he only wanted to chat over a sandwich? All this adrenaline for nothing. Eventually she got up the nerve to cross the hall and knock on his door. It opened instantly.

"Hi." A broad and contagious smile stretched across his handsome face. His eager gaze scanned her body and came to rest on her face with a deep sigh.

"Hi." Her breathing was fast and shallow. Calm down. Calm down.

They stood for a minute staring at each other, smiling like clowns. Her heart pounded in her chest. Her eyes drank him in. Every detail thrilled her. He'd styled his hair and trimmed his beard. He wore a collared button down striped shirt that looked like he'd pressed it. Nothing she saw slowed her heart rate.

"I thought you weren't home. Come in," he waved her in. "How are you doing? Is the work going okay?"

"Yeah. Sure. How about you?" She sounded like a

dummy. Her movements were jerky and her gaze jumped around his studio. Why was she so nervous?

"Are you hungry?" He led her toward the kitchen. "I made a chicken salad. I hope that's okay."

He really made lunch? Somehow that caught her by surprise. "Yes. That sounds great. Thanks."

He'd set two places at his little round table, with printed placemats and matching napkins and colourful plates. Lucy found the whole domestic thing adorable and disorienting. She had misunderstood his note after all. She'd imagined the whole thing, fuelled by Anna's provocative coaching.

He set salads and glasses of ice water in front of them."*Bon appetit.*"

After a few bites, he said, "I've given your project some thought. And I've been wondering what you'll produce at the end of it all to accomplish what you want. Are you planning to publish a paper? Or self-publish a book of your own, or what?"

Lucy chewed her salad and swallowed. "Well, I hadn't quite decided. I'd planned to present it to the department, at the university where Grandpa used to work, and Peter Sinnehauser still works. It's hard to anticipate the most effective presentation. I'm not trying to establish myself as any kind of expert in his field. That would be ridiculous." She took a bite of salad, circling her fork in the air like a pointer. "It's more like a memoir, I guess, but staking claims to his intellectual property. I guess I'm being a little sneaky since I'm an outsider. It's critical that people in his field see it."

JP leaned in, his eyes sparkling. "How about a website?

A blog. Something you can add entries to as you organize your notes."

"But who would see it? Who would know it was there?"

"That's the power of the internet. Depending on how we did it, everyone! All you'd have to do is share it on social media and send the link to anybody you wanted to read it, and there it is. In the public realm."

She sighed. "I suppose. I wouldn't have a clue where to start. All I have is a long list of chronological notes and a box of old photos."

"So the dates are important?"

"Yes. Precedence is critical to show he was doing this stuff decades before Peter worked with him or was even out of school."

JP smiled. "Finish eating. I have something to show you." He stuffed a forkful of salad in his mouth.

Her stomach flipped, putting her off her appetite, though his salad tasted great. Whatever he'd done he seemed excited about it. That meant it was good, right? Anticipation of another kind fluttered in her chest.

A while later he swept the dishes into the sink and led her to his workstation. The large L-shaped desk she'd seen in one corner of his main studio space with a bank of filing cabinets and shelves along the side wall. Above these framed artwork large and small tiled the wall. She studied it.

"Is all this your work?"

He'd sat down in front of a large computer screen and opened folders. "Yep. Here sit down beside me." He patted his extra chair.

"It's fantastic. I'm no judge of graphic design but you're so talented. This stuff is amazing."

"I used to have my own company. We did a lot more corporate design work before Fiona got sick. I sold my controlling share to my partners. Now I'm a silent partner and get a trickle of income. I do web design work now. So I can work from home."

"What are all these stickers?"

He lifted a shoulder and sighed, his eyes darting back and forth across the various framed images. "Industry awards and stuff."

Awards! Lucy looked closer at the embossed names on the labels and some framed certificates. "You're a big deal. Don't you miss all that?"

His bottom lip pushed out before he shrugged again and replaced the pensive look with his beautiful big white smile. "Sometimes. But it's worth it."

So many sacrifices. She looked at what he had opened on his screen. It looked like a website. Attractively laid out. She scanned trying to make sense of it. Why was he showing it to her?

"So this is only a mockup. I don't have any real information yet. I searched for your grandfather on the Internet and grabbed a few things to populate it. And set up a framework for you to see."

She stared at his screen, reading headings and registered the familiar images she saw there. Her mouth went dry and her stomach rolled with excitement. She brought her hand to her mouth in shock. "This is about Grandpa Henry?"

She saw his grin from the corner of her eye but couldn't tear her eyes away from the beautiful website he'd designed. "For me?"

"If you want it."

Her excitement rose. "I can insert short pieces about my research as it unfolds. I can include photographs." She could have a timeline.

"I had the idea–but I don't want to impose–but I thought if you wanted, and if it's relevant, you could put little anecdotes in here." He pointed at coloured boxes where he'd used fake Latin text to represent stories.

"You mean personal stories? So, a memoir, like I said, about the man, and his work."

He nodded. "Do you like it?"

She turned to him. He was sweet, handsome and desirable before. Suddenly in her eyes he looked like a minor god. She took his face between her hands and planted a kiss on his mouth.

He laughed, the joyful sound entering her mouth. "That's a yes?"

"That's a yes!" Without deciding to, she kissed him again, and his hands settled on her hips. Her toes curled at his touch, and her fingers thrilled at the feel of his hard planes under her fingertips. A bonus on top of his wonderful gift she filed away to appreciate later.

This time he wrapped his arms around her and kissed her back. They stopped for a second and pulled apart, their gazes raking each other's faces. They kissed again. And again. The kisses both softened and grew more intense.

Molten heat swept through her, making her shiver.

He stood up, tugging her with him and slid his hands around her back, one palm between her shoulder blades, the other slipping down to the small of her back. As he tightened his embrace, a low, needy sound emerged from his throat and he dipped his face to her shoulder. Heat swamped her body when his breath hit her skin, sending tingles out to all her fingers and toes, as their bodies aligned. He rocked his hips, pressing closer, and his excitement pressed against her belly. Her knees went weak, and as she wrapped her arms behind his neck to hold herself up, he straightened and lifted her off the floor, tilting his head to capture her mouth with his again.

She clung to him like a limpet as he deepened the kiss. This was more than a thank-you for the website.

When they came up for air, JP whispered, "Lucy? You want this as badly as I do?"

She gasped, "More badly." Her mouth flew to his neck, and her legs wrapped around him, erasing any doubts he might have.

He threw back his head and laughed aloud. He carried her into his bedroom, where he set her down and slowly, lovingly peeled her clothing from her body. Neither calm nor cool, she was never so eager to strip a man and press her hot skin along his from chest to knees, or tangle her legs with his. Jean Philippe tipped her gently back onto his bed and stopped a moment, gazing down at her, his blue eyes shadowed with desire.

"I–" He paused and knelt on the edge of the bed taking her hand. His trembled. "I haven't done this in so long. Not since…" His eyes clouded for a moment, and he shook his head as if to clear the unwelcome thoughts.

Lucy smiled, drawing her bottom her lip between her teeth. She believed he hadn't been with anyone since his wife. It surprised her in some ways, in others not. "I promise I'll be gentle."

He laughed, relaxing as she'd intended, and lowered himself beside her. She rolled toward him, pressing her body flush against his, kissing him hungrily to chase away his ghosts.

JP pressed his mouth to the crook of her neck, dragging his tongue along her collar bone, the rasp of his beard sending shivers racing along the surface of her skin like a galloping herd of wild horses. He murmured, "I don't know what I'm doing Lucy. Ever since I saw you I had to have more. I can't stay away from you."

That made two of them.

Neither of them had time to consider what they did, or why, or worry about the consequences. They came together fluidly, as if they already knew each other's bodies, each breath, caress and kiss igniting fire and whipping passion to a crescendo.

He covered her body with his questing mouth and hands, and Lucy answered by touching him everywhere, acquainting herself with each and every bulging hill and shadowed valley, the texture and scent of his skin. Crawling over each other in their eagerness, rubbing and rolling over and over questing dominance and submission in turns, clumsy and coordinated, the rest of the afternoon gave itself up to their mutual yearning and adoration. At last, they joined their bodies together, moving as one, like a single writhing beast.

SOMETIME LATER, they lay spent in his bed among the tangled sheets, their arms and legs entwined. She kissed his beautiful contoured chest, as thrilling now as their first time she'd touched it, playing the ripples of his abs with her fingertips like a harp. Now she had a long list of other favourite parts, too. He dragged his fingertips in slow motion across her shoulder and arm. They kissed again and again and again, relishing the aftershocks of their pleasure. Anna was right. This thirst must be quenched. She needed to be doing this every day. Specifically with JP and nobody else. She sighed with satisfaction.

"You are amazing," JP murmured against her hair.

She rolled onto his chest, looking up to meet his gorgeous blue eyes. "You're pretty amazing yourself." She reached up and he covered her mouth with his again. She'd taken the feel of him into herself, like breathing air, both familiar and essential to her well-being.

He flipped them onto their sides and leaned back to peer at her with affection, his eyes dancing over her features as a smile teased his sensuous lips. Her mirroring smile tugged at her cheeks, her delight was so complete.

She tried her best to ignore the inkling of worry nagging her mind because it seemed an insult to the incredible sex they'd shared. Everything about them together matched beyond perfection. Except the nagging persisted. That he'd not had a lover since his wife died a year and a half ago, and she assumed for a time before that, since Fiona would have been ill, astonished Lucy. A young, handsome and virile man had physical needs. He'd suffered a great deal of stress, worry and grief, and likely sheer fatigue since he'd lost Fiona, and he'd been caring for his kids alone. Still, he must have had opportunities.

The cynical voice in her head warned her that though he liked her, she was convenient for him, a minimal effort lover to relieve his boredom and loneliness. A little too convenient. Yet they had such a special connection. In his arms and under the heat of his gaze she felt like a beautiful, sexy woman for the first time in her life. Was this real? Something had to be wrong with this picture. She braced herself, expecting the other sneaker to drop.

It's true a relationship wasn't on her to-do list. But Anna's words of caution came back to her. When she decided one day it was time, didn't mean Mr. Right would wait for her. You had to take your moments when they came. Whatever this was with JP was without a doubt a moment.

But what about him? What did he want? What about his needs? He needed a mother for his kids. A new wife to fill the void in his life. Could Lucy handle that?

Or she could be fretting for nothing. It was possible he wanted a little company, some companionship, and the sex and nothing else.

How did Lucy prepare herself for these disparate scenarios? Playing it safe was the only course of action that made sense. That hurt her heart a little already, which meant she needed to tread on tip toes. Because all things considered, the second situation was far more likely, wasn't it?

"So, I was thinking." Lucy could hear the smile in his voice, and a hint of insecurity, and brought her focus back to his blue eyes.

"Yeeees?" If he wanted another round she was all in.

"If you'd like, you can feed me your files and I'll help you insert the text and format it on the website. Any family photos you'd like to include. Once you get in there we can talk about the layout and design elements. If you want to make changes, I can show you how. You can learn as we go and then do more on your own."

She tipped her head back to scan his face. "Are you serious? You've already done so much for me." He looked so anxious and uncertain. She touched his stubbled cheek with her fingertips, torn between crushing on his beautiful face or his gentle and generous heart. "Do you have any idea how awesome you are?"

"So what you're saying is, you like my idea?"

"I like you."

"I like you too." He glanced to the side and winced. "But please leave now."

She sat up. "What?"

"It's time to go pick up the kids."

CHAPTER SEVEN

ENTERTAINING a two-year-old didn't really prevent one's thoughts from wandering, JP realized, as he tidied the studio after dropping the kids off Friday morning. He'd been missing Lucy since the moment she'd left. His attention had drifted across the hall all day Thursday as he cared for and played with Fifi. His body wallowing in the amazing sensations echoing his time with Lucy, sore in all the right places.

He'd been fantasizing about precisely that since the moment he'd met her, but he hadn't planned to seduce her. Not like that. Not so fast! But her enthusiastic thanks tipped him over the ledge like a barrel over a waterfall, and her body pressed against his unleashed his pent up and uncontrollable desire, sending him tumbling head over keister down a cascade of sensation. JP hadn't been with a woman since Fiona got so sick she could no longer tolerate his touch. He hadn't so much as touched another woman since he'd met Fiona, over seven years ago. He thought he wasn't ready.

Was he ever wrong. His willpower was non-existent.

JP picked up Fifi's ragged stuffed rabbit, stroking its soft floppy ears with his fingertips. A shudder wracked him from head to heel, his senses awakened after a long, lonely slumber, reliving each caress of Lucy's smooth young limbs and soft curves, each luxurious kiss of her wide sensuous mouth. He swallowed, exhaling through his mouth as tingles of sensation streamed through his body, sparking a surge of lust. His dick twitched, demanding more.

His gaze settled on the photo of Fiona on the shelf, from before she got thin and weak. She used to be vibrant, laughing, her eyes sharp with intelligence and humour. But despite his devotion, specific memories of Fiona faded with each passing month. It became harder and harder to recall her touch, her scent, the sound of her voice.

Unlike Lucy, who sparkled with life, saturating his senses. Though sex with Lucy was incredible, his own motives were confused and unclear. He'd just met Lucy, and he liked everything about her, but he didn't know her well. JP wasn't looking for a real lasting relationship, so soon, was he? These things took time. Even if he liked Lucy that much, bringing a stranger into the midst of his family on a whim was risky. He wouldn't let any of them get attached to someone, and then... and then lose them. They'd only found their footing.

His gaze found Fiona's photo again, his emotions torn between devotion and desire, between loss and discovery, between the past and the present.

And if he wasn't looking for a relationship, what the hell was he doing? Using her as a fuck-buddy? Was he that kind of man? He sighed. He didn't use to be. He was a love-at-first-sight kind of guy. His new circumstances hadn't changed him that much, had they? On the other hand, he couldn't very well tolerate casual hookups to keep women separate from his kids. He definitely was not that kind of guy.

He was, however, a guy. A guy with physical needs.

But not only physical needs.

What should I do, Fi? He shook his head, fighting the tightness that grabbed his chest, the unwelcome burn in the back of his throat. He wouldn't give in to grief. Nor self-pity. He'd moved past that, for the sake of the children. Fiona was gone, he was here. This was his life. But Fiona hadn't been only his lover. She'd been his best friend. His playmate. His confidante. He wanted her back. He wished he could talk through his dilemma with her. But he couldn't.

He could confide in Lucy, though. She was young, ambitious and likely as disinterested in complicated relationships as himself. It would be a relief to her that he wasn't on the hunt for a replacement mother for his children. That couldn't be what she wanted, right? He simply could tell her how he felt. Explain his needs. She'd understand.

He'd talk to her.

By the time he finished making the beds, loading the dishwasher and tidying the studio, his resolve had disintegrated completely. Too impatient even for coy notes and chicken salad, he crossed the hall and boldly knocked on her door, his body zinging with anticipation.

She opened it right away. "Hi!"

He laughed nervously, unaccountably giddy. Thank fuck she looked happy to see him. The sight of her shot heat bubbling through his limbs. He glanced over her shoulder.

"You're alone?"

"Putting away the yoga gear." She grinned, pulling her lip between her teeth, her gaze darting, as if waiting to see what he wanted. After a beat of silence she swept her arm across the room and awkwardly tried to filled the silence. "And um, gliding my partition over, silently and um... smoothly." Their gazes locked on that word, sensual pictures swirling behind her eyes that appeared to mirror the images flashing in his own mind, and an adorable blush bloomed on her fair skin. Her gaze dropped, long dark lashes fanning her rosy cheeks, and she looked up at him uncertainly, invitingly.

His smile stretched his face tight as he let himself admire her. His gaze jumped from detail to intimate detail. Tiny freckles on the bridge of her straight nose, the way her cheeks bloomed into pink roses. The shell of her delicate ear. The places his tongue had been not long ago. She enchanted him.

At his continued silence she looked up with a question in her big eyes. He stepped closer, pulled in irresistibly, unable to escape her spell. He wanted this girl, right now. And suddenly the space between them disappeared, swallowed up in a heated kiss. His head tilted and her mouth opened to him, equally hungry. Their lips locked together as if long lost puzzle pieces, with a sigh of contentment and a needy moan. Her hands drifted over his stomach and lower. His tongue searched the silken interior of her soft mouth, the blood in his veins diving for his groin in response, his abs tightening. Her hands reached for him, sliding up his chest, reaching for his neck and fisting in his hair. She'd been remembering him, too.

AN HOUR LATER, after two rambunctious rounds of delicious sex on her window seat–how expeditiously they had dispensed with clothing–and on her futon on the floor, they dressed and crossed the hall. While he made a fresh pot of coffee, Lucy sat at his kitchen table, her eyes tracking his movements like a laser beam. He set a mug in front of her and sank into a chair. They needed to talk. That's not how he'd planned their next meeting. Whenever he was with her, his self-control vanished, his hands and mouth and dick taking on their own life without consulting his brain. He had to put the brakes on this runaway train before he was in too deep.

"What's bugging you?"

"Am I that obvious?" He took a sip of his coffee, tugged his brows and raked a hand through his hair, embarrassed. She waited, so he nodded and met her gaze. Honesty and openness were always best.

"I… How are you?"

"That's a mysteriously leading question," she smiled, her eyes teasing him for his awkwardness.

"Right. Sorry. I mean, I didn't intend to be doing this." He waved a hand back and forth between them. "Don't misunderstand me, it's great. It's wonderful!" He barked an awkward laugh and groaned inwardly at being so clumsy. Reaching across the table he took her hand, stroking her knuckles with his thumb. He really liked her. He didn't want to say anything to hurt her. "I haven't done this for a very long time. I had no one but Fiona in my life for years."

"I understand, Jean Philippe. It's okay."

"Is it though?" He met her gaze straight on. "The problem is… I mean it isn't a problem. I need to know what you expect." He winced.

She grinned and shook her head. "Not a marriage proposal, if that's what you're worried about."

He grunted, closing his eyes. "I'm sorry, Lucy. I'm being an ass. I'm adjusting here. And I'm worried about my kids, as usual. I don't want to upset the delicate balance we've achieved here. I can't afford to let them get attached to someone and…"

She nodded. "I've barely met them, JP. I'm nobody."

He cringed inwardly at her self-deprecating words. "You're not nobody. I'd like you to be somebody, though. I hate the idea of…" he paused. Were they being sneaky? Fifi was an oblivious toddler. What did his four-year-old son understand? What did he really fear?

As if she'd read his mind, she said, "Would your in-laws judge you if they knew?"

He widened his eyes. That much should be obvious. "They already assume we are." He shrugged. "No, it's the kids. I hate sneaking around. I'd like to spend more time with you. But I'm not sure…" In truth, he wasn't ready to have a romantic relationship, but he needed a break from the drudgery and loneliness. That's the promise he'd made to Fiona, and to himself. It didn't matter if he were lonely. He'd been dealt his hand. Enjoying a little sexy time was okay. But he was honour-bound to make it clear to Lucy that that's all he could offer her.

"What I want doesn't matter. It's the kids that matter.

Their security. I can't risk them getting attached to anyone else." He cringed at the sound of his words.

She huffed through her nose. "I get you're concerned about the kids. That's your priority. You're over-thinking this. Neither of us has much spare time. And, wow, it's early days for this conversation, isn't it?" She laughed, but he could tell she was trying to make it easier for him.

He nodded. Right. She was sensible, and he was paranoid. "So that's okay with you? I mean, you won't be all..." he rocked his head.

She lifted her brows.

Now he'd offended her. "Aw, Lucy. Don't take this the wrong way. It's all on me, okay? I really, really like you. A lot. I just don't know what to do."

"I'm fine, JP. I'm so enjoying our time together. I expect nothing from you."

He didn't want her to think he only wanted sex. That wasn't true. He wanted friendship, fun, connection. "I feel like, like you and I are becoming friends."

She exaggerated the nod of her head. "We are. I do consider you a friend."

In truth, he wanted that special, intimate, loving connection with someone again, someday. Life should be joyful, not sacrifice and suffering. He truly believed that. And Lucy was exactly the smart, sassy, fun and affectionate woman he'd want.

"I mean... you know, I suppose I might be ready, someday. But not right now."

She pursed her lips, the corners pulling up, amused by his awkwardness. Which was lovable.

"But I also want..." He met her gaze, his hunger for her body in the forefront of his mind.

She drew her full bottom lip between her teeth then smiled, her bedroom eyes leaving no doubt that she wanted the same thing. "So do I, JP."

"So we're good?"

"We're very good."

～

SINCE LUCY HAD IMPLICITLY AGREED NOT to hang around when JP was with his kids, to avoid confusing them, opportunities for them to be alone together came sporadically at best. Sacrificing every other workday for canoodling, wasn't practical or realistic though they had got together for lunch from time to time. And if a little canoodling resulted, well that was only because they couldn't help themselves from stealing one kiss. Sometimes a long, lingering, delicious kiss.

Like last Wednesday when she'd hit a snag formatting images in her website. She hesitated to interrupt his workday, but she'd struggled alone and come to a standstill, eventually venturing to his door and tentatively knocking. His welcome had been unconditional, however, and led to a torrent of catch-up conversation, punctuated by shy, affectionate, and increasingly hungry little touches. These led to kisses, embraces and before they knew it, a heated tumble in his bed, a shared shower afterwards, and a lingering goodbye.

After he'd helped her solve her website problems, and advanced her skills another notch, another few days went by. Lucy found it difficult to stop herself from jumping up to ask him her questions the moment they arose.

It was too easy.

Did she really need so much mentoring, or did she grab every excuse to be near him again? This kind of need—was it dependence?–didn't sit well with her. For better or worse, Grandpa's constant scrutiny of her friends, particularly her male friends, had taught her to depend on no one, need no one. She'd learned to be all right on her own.

She made headway. She'd organized her files. A structure for her presentation emerged, aided in large part by the supportive, creative and easy to navigate architecture of the website template JP had designed for her. He was so talented, as she increasingly realized, and gave thanks for, every day. The basic landing page was ready to go live, though not all the pages were yet ready to share. With anyone except JP. She was eager to share every milestone with him and yet held back.

When weakness overcame her, he'd knock on her door.

"Got a sec?" he'd say with a mischievous grin, triggering an eddy of excitement in her belly. "I want to show you something." The something would invariably be something sweet, silly or insignificant. A drawing brought home by Christian, a funny snap on his phone of something cute that Fifi had done, an esoteric Dr. Who question, or a new logo he'd designed and wanted her opinion on–as if her opinion counted. Ultimately an excuse to share a cup of coffee, news of the day, a laugh, a kiss, a caress. And sometimes, another turn in his wrinkled sheets. She came to look forward to the interruptions and expect them as her new normal.

Every time JP invited her for lunch, or she knocked on his door with a question about her website, the temptation proved irresistible. Jean Philippe was trying as much as she was to reign in their desire for each other and equally failing. Perhaps JP held himself back even more than Lucy did. Or perhaps it only felt that way to Lucy, whose obsession with the man grew daily.

Her admiration and desire raised her own defences. Surely she was the one getting involved in something she couldn't handle. Questions kept arising for her, about what Grandpa Henry would think, what he would say or do, about JP and this situation in which they found themselves. Was Lucy being a fool? Was JP worthy of her thoughts? Her mind kept searching for the flaws and problems. The only problem she had was craving more.

What would Grandpa say about JP's aloof manner when they crossed paths on Sundays as his in-laws brought the kids home? The fact that, despite their best efforts, the kids themselves grew accustomed to her didn't help. While the in-laws glowered judgementally, JP fumbled awkwardly, and Lucy looked on, knowing full well that their suspicions were true. Christian babbled to Lucy about his week as though she were part of the family, and even Fifi had grown confident enough to waddle over and grab her leg, demanding to be picked up.

Lucy took to dashing into her studio before any chance encounter occurred, to avoid the confusion, bristling silently behind her own door at what she imagined happened beyond his.

During the week, awareness of the time he spent with his kids, coming and going, familiar sounds of their domesticity wafting across the hall, permeated her consciousness, a pang of longing, resistance and even, sadly, resentment building up in the space between them like a wall. It was all in her mind, which obsessed on the thing it couldn't have. She hadn't studied psychology for nothing. But it didn't make the feelings vanish.

They were neighbours and friends, not only lovers. She didn't want every encounter to end up with them in bed together. That would be unhealthy. For Lucy, self-preservation was her goal as much as the necessity to ensure she actually got her work done every day.

Her time was as tight and her goals as ambitious as ever, and now she had a harder time concentrating. Her email exchanges with Peter Sinnehauser and other staff at the department confused her. Despite keeping her posted on his ambitious publication schedule, he seemed happy to hear from her and answer her questions, eager to talk about Grandpa Henry. She couldn't decide if he gloated, or was oblivious to the damage he'd inflict if he took credit for her dear grandfather's lifetime of hard work.

Grandpa Henry's research interested to her, but not so engrossing as to keep her mind from wandering to JP. JP's smiling face, his ready laugh, his rippling muscles, his tender and passionate lovemaking. In fact it pushing those thoughts and the associated echoes of emotion and sensation from her mind became increasingly difficult. The memory of Jean Philippe's caressing fingertips and hot seeking mouth caused Lucy's thoughts to go on a cross-country tour, tingles and shivers wracking her body as she stared into space.

CHAPTER EIGHT

AT THE WEEKLY touch football game Saturday afternoon, JP was painfully conscious that Mark and the other guys' wives and girlfriends were there to cheer and chat with each other. This was something Fiona sometimes used to do, but rarely. She preferred to stay home with the kids, or take them to visit her parents. He'd never resented her introversion, or need to spend time alone.

Afterwards, when they were gathered at the pub, he felt conspicuously alone and outcast. JP sensed that Lucy would fit in with his crowd and would enjoy these weekend forays into careless fun and sociability. More and more, he wished he could bring her and introduce her to his oldest friends.

A clap on the back brought him out of his ruminations.

"Hey, man," Mark said. "Where'd you go?"

JP shook it off. "Just inside my head too much."

"You doin' okay?" His grip on JP's shoulder tightened. Mark understood JPs moods. He'd been JP's closest friend since college, his colleague at work, and now his sometimes client. He'd also, next to JP's family, been the biggest support during Fiona's illness and after her death. He didn't really have secrets from Mark.

He nodded. He wanted to confide in him. He wanted to tell him, tell someone, all about Lucy and what a treasure she was. How light and joyful she made him feel. What had been happening in his life, inside of him, these past days and weeks. It felt important, even though he didn't know what to do about it all.

But if he talked about Lucy... well that would make it all official. She'd be an undeniable part of his life. Too real. And then he'd have to figure out what it was, and what to do about it. These people knew Fiona. Would his friends think that he'd betrayed her memory somehow? Would they think he'd moved on too soon? Would they understand how important Lucy had become to him?

"Yeah. I'm good actually. Thanks. Just not in the mood for this tonight. I think I'll head home early and get some rest."

And he did, and when he got there, he went straight to Lucy's door and knocked. And she opened it, welcoming him into her arms. And then everything was all right again, though they didn't get any rest at all.

And he still didn't know what to do about it.

DESPITE THEIR BEST INTENTIONS, mutual attraction was getting the better of them. Saturdays became a treat that Lucy looked forward to—the highlight of her week, in truth because they had more time together, uninterrupted by his need to be a dad, or by work.

JP continued joining his friends for their weekly touch football games with a beer or two afterwards, though he'd never invited her to join them. Then while Christian and Fifi spent the rest of their weekly twenty-four hours with their grandparents, JP and Lucy indulged in leisurely evenings with wine and Dr. Who episodes, followed by luxurious, unhurried lovemaking.

Sometimes quick, hard, urgent lovemaking before the wine and Dr. Who, and then half-hearted video-watching, with drowsy naps and more lovemaking afterwards. Then, without fail, he always gently sent her home so they could get a good sleep and he could wake up early, get his shopping done and resume his fatherly duties the next day.

Admittedly, there were a couple of times when, in the aftermath of a particularly world-rocking orgasm, they'd fallen asleep in each other's arms and Lucy had awoken and tiptoed out in the middle of the night. And they may have crossed paths in the laundry room a time or two on Sunday mornings.

She respected his wishes and wanted to help him maintain his routine, even though there was a small part of her that felt like an outcast and resented having to sneak around and slink out in the night like a criminal. But, she chided herself, that was being immature and petty.

A couple of weeks later, JP returned from the bar later than usual, a little drunk and still dirty and dressed in his sweaty football gear. He knocked on her door, and when she opened met her with a sheepish smile.

Slumped against her door jamb, loose limbed and grinning, he still managed to be adorable and sexy despite stinking like a barnyard animal.

She shook her head, smiling at him. After all, she had no expectations.

"Sorry, *cheri*. I'll just grab a shower, 'kay?" Then he promptly lost his balance and nearly tripped and fell over, if Lucy hadn't grabbed his arm.

She laughed. "How about I help you get to the shower, funny guy?" She escorted him across the hall and helped him insert the key in his lock. "What happened today? A little extra time in the pub?"

"Yeah, yeah." His speech was lazy and slow. "Today we played in a fun tournament with a few other teams. Took longer. We won, so..."

"So you had to celebrate. I get it." She led him to his bathroom and helped him peel off his stinky stiff clothes. "I hope you didn't drive home."

"Nah. Simon drove my car."

JP stood, leaning his hip against the bathroom vanity, grinning at her, the shower forgotten. "S'nice to see you, sweetheart."

"Okay." She turned on and adjusted the shower and gently shoved him in, where he rested his head against the tile wall under the stream of hot water for several minutes. "Did you fall asleep?"

"Ugh. No." He was gradually coming to his senses. He roughly scrubbed his face with both hands.

She couldn't resist. He looked amazing standing there with the water sluicing down his long limbs and rippled abs, completely unselfconscious. Lucy reached in and took the bar of soap, sliding it over his beautiful, muscled back, shoulders and arms, working up a lather, indulging in the look and luscious texture of his gleaming wet skin. Familiar tingles raced through her body, awakening the powerful desire that the mere thought of this man now stimulated in her blood. She watched him harden and stand up. Her stomach tightened as arrows of lust shot down to her core. She paused in her washing, shuddering, her slippery hand on his hard stomach.

It tightened and JP stirred at last, turning his head to direct his hot blue gaze her way. "Get in here, beautiful."

She swallowed, not needing a second invitation. Rinsing and drying her hands, she stripped out of her own clothes in micro-seconds and stepped into his open arms. Under the stream of hot water, she pressed her aching needy body against his wet soapy skin with a shiver that shook her from ears to toes.

His arms slid around her in a caressing cage. He bent to capture her mouth with his, hot water accompanying his tongue as it dove into her mouth with fervour and his arms tightened around her. His strong hands slid down her wet back, fingertips digging into her skin, and gripping her butt cheeks, pulling her against the rigid erection that he'd turned to press against her with a deep hungry moan. With a little help, it slipped from pressing into her stomach to between her legs, and she brought her thighs together to hug his thick shaft, wishing it inside of her. Deep inside her.

"Jean Philippe," she croaked, her voice hoarse with need. In answer, he slid one hand down the crack of her butt and slid his middle finger inside her. She pressed her open mouth against his wet neck, licking his skin, sliding her tongue down his gorgeous pecs while her hands slipped down and gripped his shaft, hard.

"I know what you want." He spun her around, guiding her hands to the tile wall and digging his fingertips into her waist so she wouldn't slip. Within seconds he buried himself inside her with a long shuddering groan, giving her exactly what she wanted, their shared moans and screams rising and bouncing off of the tiled walls as hot water continued to stream down around them.

With limbs as pliant as wires, they quickly dried each other off and tumbled into his bed. Something about the sensuality of the shower kicked their desire into high gear. Once wasn't enough. Twice wasn't enough. Tonight, they explored each other's bodies thoroughly and with abandon, experimenting with new ways to stimulate and satisfy each other, rising to new transcendent heights of desire and rapture. They didn't stop for food or drink, they skipped Dr. Who, and lost themselves in loving each other late into the night.

CHAPTER NINE

Loud, insistent banging woke them with a start. JP sat bolt upright, the sheets falling away from his bare chest and pulling away from hers. Lucy's heart hammered against her ribcage in a rapid echo of the thumping coming from his front door.

"*Sacré bleu!* What the hell time is it?" His head whipped back and forth, searching.

"Hello? Hello? John Philip, are you there?" Muffled voices filtered through the door. "Not again. Can't the man tell time? We arrive at exactly the same time each week!"

Lucy leaned over to look at his bedside alarm clock. The numbers barely registered on her tired brain, they made so little sense.

"After... twelve?"

"What!" Before Lucy's thoughts cleared, JP leapt from the bed in a frenzy and yanked on whatever discarded clothing his hands found

She sat up, picking up the clock and shaking it, disbelieving. How could they have slept through the morning completely? Dead to the world. Oblivious of passing time. Surely this was wrong. "Uh…"

JP scrabbled and ran for the door then paused, looking back at her, his eyes wide with panic. Baggy sweat pants and a striped dress shirt that he'd buttoned wrong, the fabric pulling to catch up. His hair standing up straight on one side. He looked ridiculous. She stood up and went to him has he paused in the bedroom doorway.

"You've missed." She reached for his shirt to correct the misaligned buttons, but he swatted her hands away, impatient and uncaring.

His eyes finally clearing of sleep and confusion, his blue gaze locked on hers and he hissed, "You've got to hide!"

"What?"

"Please! They can't see you here." With no further explanation, he ran to the entry door to let his in-laws and children in.

Unclear whether she was hiding from the in-laws, his children, or both, Lucy dipped into the bathroom after giving his closet a dismissive glance. She would not hide in a closet for anyone. She'd had the presence of mind to close the bedroom door. Her own clothes remained piled on the bathroom floor, so she put them on. Though they'd started last night with a long shower, she wished for another one, to rinse away the sweat and grit and scents of a long night of sex, but daren't run water to wash. So she sat on the closed toilet seat and waited, straining to hear through the closed doors.

After uncountable minutes of murmuring voices, she heard a door thud closed. Then the sound of footsteps moving toward her. Expecting JP, she already had a sheepish smile on her face awaiting him as the bathroom door swung open.

Except it wasn't JP.

Her gaze swung down to meet the curious blue eyes of Christian, who'd paused in the bathroom doorway, puzzled to find her there.

"Um. Hello, Christian." Lucy smoothed a hand over her hair, imagining she looked about as disheveled as JP had upon waking.

"Hi, Lucy." He continued to stare at her for a long minute or two, and finally blinked and said. "I have to go wee-wee." His head tilted, as though trying to figure out how to achieve this goal while she sat on the toilet.

"Ah. I'm sorry, sweetheart. Come on." She stood up.

Before she could leave the room, or even think to turn and help him, he'd flipped up the lid, dropped his drawers and hauled his little butt up onto the toilet. A tiny tinkling sound began.

She stared at him. Of course he was completely unself-conscious. Obviously he was used to having adults around while he did his business. And she was no different. Except she was. But he didn't seem to think so or mind if she stood there watching him. She shuffled back to peek out of the bathroom door.

"Are your grandparents gone?"

"Yup." Tinkle, tinkle.

"Er. How was your visit this weekend?"

"Okay. What did you do?" Tinkle, tinkle.

Apparently tiny penises didn't mean tiny bladders. How did she answer that? What did he think about finding her in his father's bathroom in the middle of the day? She decided not to answer.

"What's your dad doing?"

His little shoulders came up to his ears in silence.

She nodded. Okay. Should she leave? Stay? Call out?

Before she had to figure that out, the bathroom door swung wide. "Christian?"

They both looked up to see JP blinking at the scene, his eyes wide, his mouth pressed into a tight thin line. Lucy crossed her arms over her chest.

"Can you wipe me, please?" Christian's little voice broke the silence.

He was looking at her. She swung her gaze to JP's, uncertain what was expected of her. "Um…"

JP cleared his throat. "Can you excuse us for a moment?"

She nodded and left quickly, then found herself standing in the middle of the disheveled bedroom, ghost images of their long night of passion flashing behind her lids, no idea if he'd want her to be discovered by Fifi also or to stay put.

Where was Fifi? Lucy stepped silently to the bedroom door which sat ajar and peeked out. Fifi lay on the sofa wrapped in a blanket, clutching her rabbit and sucking her thumb, unaware of the drama unfolding in Lucy's heart. She was about to tip-toe out into the main studio when she heard soft voices.

"Why's Lucy here, Papa?"

"Uh… here, stand up."

There were scuffling noises, and then a flush. Through the rush of running water Christian's firm, high-pitched interrogation continued.

"Your hair's funny. Did you jus' wake up?"

"Uh… yeah. Yes. Sorry bud. Slept in today."

"Did Lucy sleep over? Grandma thought you weren't home."

"What? No! Nah. What a crazy idea."

Lucy's heart pinched and dropped to her stomach.

"Do you like Lucy, Papa? I like Lucy. Is Lucy gonna be our new mom?"

An expectant pause followed, and Lucy held her breath. She oughtn't to be eavesdropping, but every cell in her body stretched toward the conversation beyond the door, desperate to know what Jean Philippe would say next.

"Wha–? That's crazy, C. Of course not. Lucy's not family. We hardly know her. How could you ask that?"

Everything froze. Her heart stopped beating. A process of calcification began as his cold words seeped into her chest and wrapped around it, slowly turning it to stone.

"But…" A long pause followed as he puzzled something out in his four-year-old brain. Christian's voice was tiny, barely audible. "Is that why you make us go to Grandma's? So Lucy can come over?"

"No, no, darling, Christian." She heard kissing noises. "I miss you terribly when you're gone to Grandma's. Lucy… Lucy's keeps me company while you're away, love. So I'm not too lonely without you!"

There came the rustle of fabric, a briefly running tap, more rustling. "There you go, bud."

"I wanna stay with Lucy too, Papa. Did she go home?"

"Uuh…"

Lucy took a step back, found herself trapped between the two rooms, uncertain which way to go, but he didn't immediately appear. Lucy wondered if he felt anything then, realizing that she might have overheard, if it even occurred to him how much his words hurt her. If he even cared.

The bathroom door opened and JP stepped out, his gaze scanning the room. It caught on hers, staring back at him, afraid to speak, unsure what he wanted her to do.

"Hey! Lucy! You're still here." JP opened the door to let Christian follow him out into the bedroom. His gaze darted around at the messy bed, the clothing and pillow strewn floor, anywhere but at her, sighing and raking a hand through his hair. "Wow. Wow. What a mess."

She swallowed, her muscles tight. She didn't think he was referring to the tumbled room. Noticing Christian standing and staring up at her, a confusion still in his eyes, she offered a tight smile. "Well, I should get going, I guess. Um, thanks?"

JP nodded, rubbing the back of his neck roughly up and down and Lucy noted his tension and discomfort. What had happened to her lover? Where had he gone? She watched his face pull tight as he twisted his wedding band nervously, staring at the top of Christian's head.

He wouldn't meet her gaze, and that alone hit her like a knife to the heart, when as the sun rose a few hours ago, they'd seen into each other's eyes, and hearts, with a raw, naked honesty that was incomparable.

"Yes. Yes. Thanks for dropping by. And uh, thanks for returning the... uh, thing..." He shuffled his bare feet on the smooth wooden floor planks. His hand darted out and snatched the empty Dr. Who DVD case that sat on his dresser. They'd watched a little of their favourite episode, the Two Doctors, while they ate a snack in the middle of the night. His breath puffed out, and he waved the case back and forth like a flag of truce. "... the uh, DVD you borrowed. I'll send you a text later, yeah?" His glance flew over her shoulder like a dart and stuck on the door frame behind her, as though begging her to disappear through it. There was no one here but them and Christian. Why couldn't he look at her? He couldn't have made his wishes any clearer. When it came to his kids, to his family, there was no place for her.

He'd dismissed their special night together like a fast food treat, a cheap bag of chips, quickly and carelessly consumed, the wrapper scrunched and discarded thoughtlessly. Though his words were baffling and irrelevant, every twitch of muscle, darting glance, and defensive posture screamed at her. This was textbook discomfort, embarrassment, withdrawal... rejection.

She stared at him, her limbs weak, her heart slowly cracking into little shards, crumbling to the floor like a smashed fossil. She knew what they'd set out to do a few weeks ago. What they'd said they were doing. But last night... last night changed all of that.

At least she'd thought it had.

After their night together, so fraught with passion, so completely consuming, heart-wrenching in its tenderness and deep uninhibited intimacy, his cool, dismissive manner smashed through her heart like a sledgehammer, destroying something tender and raw and vulnerable that she'd laid open for him. How could he dismiss her so coldly? Was he so embarrassed by her? Did he feel so little?

Her mouth fell ajar, then snapped tight as she felt her chin quiver. Her breath stopped in her tight throat, her stomach clenching at the realization. You fool, Lucy! You fool. This wasn't what you thought it was. He's not here for you. He's not available to love you back. He's not who you wanted him to be.

What would Grandpa Henry say to her now?

Before the tears that burned her eyes and throat escaped, she pushed her tight cheeks into a miserable facsimile of a smile and raised a hand in farewell. "Right! Okay, well. I'll catch up with you later, JP. Bye, Christian. Enjoy your Sunday, guys." She spun on her heel and fled, racing for the door without even glancing back to see if Fifi noticed her, or if JP followed her. It didn't matter, anyway.

He wasn't what she thought he was. He'd failed Grandpa Henry's criteria for honour, honesty, sensitivity. And courage. He'd failed her. He'd broken her heart.

JEAN PHILIPPE WISHED he could have knocked on Lucy's door immediately but the kids demanded his attention. Her sudden departure left him blinking and shaking his head, starting and stopping various chores. Why did she leave so abruptly? Couldn't she have hung around for a cup of coffee at least? He started making the bed, then left it to check on Fifi, who was listless and dozing on the sofa, sucking her thumb. Bending to kiss her soft, domed forehead, he picked up the kids bags and went to sort dirty from clean laundry, then left that half finished to check the fridge for supplies.

He wanted to go to her, but the kids needed him. He dragged the kids out with him to do his weekly shopping, because that hadn't happened in the morning, though shopping with toddlers in tow was profoundly inefficient and frustrating. Fifi didn't appreciate being dragged to the store and had a huge meltdown right there in the super-market. Afterwards, frazzled, tired and cross with each other, they returned home for a snack and a nap. When the kids were both asleep, he texted Lucy again, but she didn't reply. Had she gone out, too?

His update to Maman, on the other hand, elicited a quick text in response

I'll see if I can get a flight out.

He sighed. He hated to cause her so much inconve-nience, but he had to admit he was on his last legs. Though his recent weeks with Lucy had been wonderful, he real-ized his sleep had suffered, and consequently his energy, his patience, and his mental powers.

As usual, after a visit with the grandparents, Christian bubbled over with stories to share. Though from JP's perspective, one visit sounded much like the other, he supposed being away from his father for twenty-four hours made everything seem notable to Christian, so he had to share it, and JP encouraged him. In truth he spent so much time alone with his children that he almost wanted to tell them his news as well. He had no one else to talk to, really.

Fifi got increasingly cranky, refusing to eat. He hoped Maman could come.

"What did you eat at Grandma's?" he asked Christian, but got no useful information. They both drooped, more than ready for bed by seven-thirty.

Several more texts to Lucy in the evening, and through his busy catch-up day on Monday went unanswered, leaving him in a permanent state of obsessive worry about what was wrong. He couldn't stop thinking about her, her sudden withdrawal, the strange look on her face as she left.

Saturday night had been epic, extraordinary, and life changing. Is that why she left? Did their intense connection scare her? Or did he completely misread the situation?

He couldn't believe they'd poured so much into loving each other, with such intensity and whole-heartedness, that they'd utterly drained themselves and slept until noon. What a shit show! If he were going to introduce another woman to his nit-picking and grieving in-laws, which he supposed one day he would, he wanted to do it on his own terms. Certainly not like that, caught, literally, with his pants down.

He continued to worry and obsess through a series of client meetings and a project deadline that took most of Monday. When he had a few spare minutes in between, he popped out into the hall to knock on her door. He stood, waiting, tapping his lip with his fingertips, expecting her footsteps, her smiling face, any moment. He listened at the door, but learned nothing. Still no answer, no acknowledgement of any kind. Either she was nose to the grindstone (but why ignore him?) or gone out somewhere.

What was going on? Had he done something to piss her off? Was she ghosting him? What was he not getting here?

Saturday night had shaken him to the soles of his feet. And Sunday hadn't really given them a chance to process their feelings. To JP, their relationship had catapulted three levels overnight. In truth, what he was feeling didn't come on over one night, however intense, passionate and raw that experience might have been. Whatever that meant, they had to talk about it. He was terrified and didn't know what to do next.

Scrawling a quick note, he slipped it under her door.

This feeling had been growing since that first day they'd met, when she'd caught him spying. Though he'd begun with mere curiosity about the squeaking noise, the moment he saw her, something grabbed him in the gut. There was something about Lucy that penetrated his armour and awoke his sleeping soul. Something about her that made him suddenly want more, more life, more living, his promises be damned. His brain was spinning, rewriting all the rules he'd made for himself, creating new justifications and rationales.

He didn't know what it meant, but he couldn't ignore his feelings any more.

He'd try to catch her after her evening yoga class, if the kids gave him a minute of peace.

JP struggled through the evening, making a simple supper for himself and the kids. Fifi still refused to eat, only drinking milk, her crankiness and lethargy increasing as it got closer to bedtime. To him she seemed flushed and overly warm. Had she had something to eat yesterday at Angus and Maeve's that didn't agree with her? Or was she coming down with a bug?

Despite seeming tired, when he went to tuck Fifi in, she squirmed and whimpered and fussed, and he had to lie down with her for a while to settle her down, aware that Lucy's class would be ending soon. He strained his ears for voices in the hall.

Just after eight, when he thought he heard a muffled conversation, he carefully extracted himself from the lightly dozing children and tiptoed to his studio door.

Opening it as silently as possible, he stepped out just in time to see Lucy's door closing, clipping the end off of a conversation between herself and a woman friend, probably Anna. He sighed. His opportunity to talk to her tonight was lost.

CHAPTER TEN

LUCY DIDN'T NEED to ask Anna to stay after evening yoga on Monday. She followed Lucy in silence back into the studio after the others had left, closing the door behind her.

"Cup of tea?" Lucy asked, wary.

They curled up as usual among the blankets and blocks on the wide platform under the window that spanned the width of the room, overlooking the back lane with its brick wall and blue dumpsters. This place had come to feel like home, though she knew it was temporary.

"My time here is half over."

Anna peered at her, concern and questions swimming in the look she shot over the lip of her mug, saying nothing.

Lucy shook her head. "The funny thing is… I always believed it was a short-term, superficial thing. Didn't I always say so?"

Anna hummed.

"It's only lately that I got sucked into believing something more was going on."

Anna's nodded, as though she feared knocking Lucy off her balance and breaking her stride.

"It's just lust, right? The oxytocin is affecting my brain function. Everything got distorted. I mean, it's been a long time since I've had any kind of regular sex…"

Anna's brows curled down at the outside, and she tilted her head to the side. Her expression looked remarkably like sympathy, and Lucy's throat tightened, making her next words sound gurgle-y and thick. "Same for him. All alone these past two years." Her chin trembled. "The sex was superb."

Anna reached forward with one hand and gripped Lucy's, her gaze wavering between Lucy's quivering lips and tearing eyes. Lucy didn't intend to cry. She'd already cried all the tears.

She had to be pragmatic. "He doesn't really want me, Anna. I was just…" she waved her hand at the door. "… convenient." The last word emerged as a squeak that stretched into a long pitiful whine. "He doesn't wa-ant me, Anna."

Anna set down her mug and wrapped her arms around Lucy's slumping shoulders, pulling her in for a tight hug, rocking her back and forth until her crying jag ran its course. Lucy slumped, her limbs heavy, her chest tight as a *pasasana*, the noose of wrapped limbs squeezing the air from her lungs.

When she had no more tears to cry, and felt calmer, Anna refreshed their teacups.

"He's just not available emotionally. I was a fool to forget that. He told me so right from the start, didn't he?"

"Hm. It sounded like things changed. He seemed invested."

Lucy nodded. She handed Anna the note. "He slipped this under my door this afternoon.

Anna took it and read it, Lucy watching her read the words she'd read a hundred times, memorized, trying to decipher its cryptic meaning.

Hey! Where'd you go?

Can we hang out?

I need to see you. JP

Anna shrugged. "This could mean anything."

Or nothing. He seemed unaware of what he'd done.

"You're making a mountain out of a molehill."

"That's what I'm afraid of," Lucy replied.

"Tell me again what happened on Sunday afternoon."

Lucy did. Each time she reviewed it, she felt more like the small, worthless girl who's family ignored and shunted her aside. Hopeless about the imagined intensity of their last night together.

"Let me get this straight, girl. He hasn't cut you loose. He's not the one who's stopped communicating, right?"

Lucy swallowed. "That's not the point. He... he turned his back on me. He closed that door."

"Sensitive, aren't you? I'm not surprised you've had no long-term relationships, with that attitude."

Lucy's head jerked up. "What?"

"You expect too much of people. Nobody's perfect. What did terrible thing did JP do?"

"He betrayed me! He denied me to my face."

"Oh, Lucy, Lucy. I'm afraid your beloved Grandfather ruined you. Was he such an amazing, flawless specimen of manhood that nobody will ever compare?"

"He was wonderful."

"Tell me something Henry did that JP didn't."

"He stood by me, always. No matter what."

"You know what I think of that. What else?"

"Henry was generous. He gave me thoughtful gifts that showed me he cared and understood me. He paid attention to what was important to me."

Anna twisted her mouth, considering. "JP designed that website for you and taught you how to edit it, didn't he?"

Lucy nodded. "Henry was so caring. Always looking out for me. He brought me treats."

"Hasn't JP fed you? Helped you in a thousand ways?" Anna gestured to the rolling screen that still divided the studio space after yoga class.

Lucy shrugged, refusing to acknowledge that JP could compare to Grandpa Henry in that department. "Grandpa was honest, and hardworking, smart and funny..." JP's accomplishments flashed in her mind with each word like a slideshow. His design talent, his resourcefulness and sacrifice working from home to care for his kids, the self-less way he nursed Fiona when she was sick. Lucy could think of no other attribute that Jean Philippe didn't share, their joyful times together, however stolen and illicit, flashing in her mind. But... "Grandpa was loyal."

"JP is loyal. To his dead wife's wishes. To his kids. To his in-laws, no matter how badly they treat him." Anna's steady gaze met and held Lucy's. "It's only you that have got short shrift. I think your ego's bruised."

"Why are you being so mean?" Lucy dropped her gaze to her hands. "Grandpa was courageous. He always faced the truth, never hid from it. He would never have done that." Her heart squeezed, reliving the crushing sense of rejection JP's blank dismissal caused. "He was a gentleman."

No one compared to Grandpa Henry. He was incomparable. Lucy pushed away the little voice that said this was her problem. No living man could ever fill the ideal space that her lost, beloved grandpa filled in her heart and in her life. She was a trained psychologist. She knew this. But the knowledge didn't assuage the hurt she experienced at Jean Philippe's cold denial. She wanted someone to love her like that again, wholly and unconditionally. Was that such a bad thing?

"What's so ungentlemanly about preserving your privacy and dignity, Lucy?" Anna's head shook side-to-side. "He's torn. You're not giving the poor guy enough time to process his feelings. You said yourself it's been a whirlwind."

"I don't know, Anna."

Anna took her leave, Lucy seeing her to the door, watching her walk away toward the elevator. Alone again, she stood in the corridor, staring at Jean Philippe's closed and quiet door.

Sighing, she turned toward her temporary home, wishing her brief sabbatical and tenure here could end so she could return to her normal life and forget him. Her door almost closed when she heard his agitated voice.

"Lucy!"

Her belly fluttered. She glanced over her shoulder.

JP stood in his open doorway. His unshaven, tense face showed confusion, hurt and yearning to match her own.

"Lucy?"

She swallowed, her mouth dry as dust. She almost slammed the door, her breathing shallow, and bees buzzing in her head, unable to face him and his expression. She shook her head. A snake coiled in the pit of her stomach, leaving her nauseous. So handsome and dear. So inconstant. So dangerous.

He stepped toward her, crossing the hall halfway. "What's going on? Why won't you talk to me?"

But it wouldn't work. No matter what they both felt. The endorphin haze had them in its grip. Soon enough, he'd remember his commitments and obligations. He'd said he didn't date or want a new relationship to interfere with his family life. He didn't want her to be a part of that.

Even if he'd faltered, he'd soon come to his senses. He'd have to choose. And he'd choose his kids. He would. And where would that leave her? Foolish girl. In her heart she realized she grasped at reasons to reject him to protect herself. Because he'd reject her again, once and for all.

"It's best to end it, cold."

JP's brow folded, darkening his blue gaze to indigo. "What? Why?"

She jiggled her head, tense and unhappy to have to explain the obvious. "This isn't going anywhere, JP."

"I beg to differ. What about Saturday? This is going somewhere, Lucy. I don't know where, but somewhere. Don't shut me out. We have to talk."

"No. You know in your heart what you want." Her voice rose, and she tamped it down, hissing. "Where your priorities lay. We just forgot for a moment…"

"No!"

"Shh." She glanced down the hall, a burning heat pressing behind her eyes. "Come on. We lost perspective. You saw the truth on Sunday. You're the one that shut me out, Jean Philippe. That's why you lied to Christian."

For a second he looked confused, a frown flickering across his brow. "No Lucy! That's not... I panicked, that's all. He's four. I didn't know how to explain. But when you left I..." He stopped, lifting one shoulder, his mouth moving as his gaze swung over her face, tracing her features one by one, as though he hadn't seen her for years.

She pulled her lips in, pinching them together enough for the sharp pain to chase off the trembling that threatened to reveal her mounting emotions. "I did the right thing. I admit, things got intense–"

"You think?" he croaked.

She ignored his incredulous glare, keeping her gaze down. She forced words past the tightness in her chest that crushed the air from her. Liar. Liar. "We agreed it would be a short-term fling, right? I've got a deadline. You've got your kids and work." She spoke the truth, though she left out part of it. A thought that had somehow got lost beneath all the madness pushed its way to the front, putting everything into a perspective of sorts.

I love you!

She couldn't hold his gaze, swallowing to moisten her dry throat, glancing up and down the hall. No neighbours stirred at this late hour. "It was great. You're a super guy, JP. But it's over now."

"Please don't do this. Lucy, I'm sorry if I hurt your feelings on Sunday. But let's talk it out."

No!

"It's over. I'm sorry. This is what's best."

His feet remained frozen in the middle of the hall, but he lifted one hand toward her, stopped and let it fall. His mouth moved, the shape of her name, but he made no sound.

Her head moved of its own accord, back and forth, back and forth, while she stepped back and closed her door, leaving him standing there alone. Her heart broke, inch by inch as the door cut him from her view, from her life.

Just before the door severed the last bit of shared air between them, she whispered, "Thank you for designing my website, Jean Philippe. You're a great guy. I'm sorry."

Her voice caught on the last word, choking it off, before the door latched closed. She turned the deadbolt, dipped her forehead to the wood, and let loose her tears.

CHAPTER ELEVEN

BANG, bang, bang!

Lucy awoke from a deep, exhausted sleep.

Groggy, she shuffled to the kitchen and flicked on a light, trying to decipher the racket and determine its source.

Bang, bang, bang!

At first it seemed to be coming from the corridor outside, but now someone was definitely banging on her door.

"Lucy!"

Jean Philippe! Hesitating only a half a heartbeat to wonder why he was here, she slid open the lock. Her pulse racketed against her ribs. Had he seen through her pitiful lies? Was he feeling as desperately lonely without her as she was without him and come to beg her to change her mind?

Peering out, the sight that met her bleary eyes caused cold dread to flood her limbs. Suddenly she was terrifyingly wide awake. JP stood with Fifi in his arms, his bearded face haggard, his eyes wild and dark. Fifi was mostly naked, her pudgy limbs hanging limply.

Her heart slammed in her chest. Oh, my God! "What's going on?"

"We're going... hospital," he croaked. "Fifi's temperature's too high and won't come down."

He stood too close. Lucy felt heat radiating off of them and smelled sweat and fear and a faint trace of urine.

She glanced down at Fifi, her eyes widening as she took in the dark hair wetly plastered to her domed forehead. Fifi made no sound at all, not even a whimper. One tiny bright red ear and flushed cheek showed, the other side of her face squashed against JP's heaving chest. "How high?" Her voice came out shrill, her dry throat choking the words.

"Over one hundred five."

"What is it?" She knew so little about children.

"I don't know." His hoarse voice was grim, matching his fearful expression. "I think it's been creeping up since Sunday afternoon. I didn't realize at first and it just shot up."

His strong arms wrapped tightly around his daughter, her sweaty bare arms and legs splayed. She looked so vulnerable. He looked so helpless. "Do you need a ride to the hospital?"

"Mark's on his way. He lives close by." He lifted his frantic blue gaze at last to peer into her face, and she read all his terror and need. "Christian's still half asleep. I don't want to drag him out of bed and I don't want to upset him either." He gripped her upper arm, his hand taut. "Stay with him, please? You can go back to sleep, just be there with him?"

"Of course! Yes."

"I'm sorry to trouble you, but we have to go right now."

Lucy felt hurt that he would even say that, but it was understandable. She could only shake her head in denial. She would do anything for him. Reaching forward, she took his anguished face between her palms, searching his eyes with her own. "It'll be okay, Jean Philippe. Stay calm." She stroked his cheeks, trying to soothe him, though her own heart squeezed with panic. She let one hand drop gently to Fifi's damp head and her pulse kicked with terror at the intense heat. But she hid her fear. "She'll be okay. She has to be."

"Oh! My mother is arriving this morning. She was on her way for a visit already so she's in transit. I couldn't reach her," he said. "If you can meet her and explain? I'll get back here as soon as I can."

"Don't worry, Jean Philippe. I'll be here. I'll take care of everything. Just go!"

He loped down the hall, his long legs eating up the space in seconds, and dove downstairs, disappearing from her sight. She glanced across the hall where he'd left his door wide open. She swallowed, breathing through her mouth, gathering her thoughts. Shaking her head to clear it, she stepped back into her studio, grabbed some yoga clothes, a hair brush, her phone and her keys. She locked her own door and went over to JP's studio. Peeking in the bedroom, she saw that Christian was indeed still asleep, his cheeks flushed, his ruddy hair fluffed, one pale leg thrown over the covers.

The studio was in shambles. Blankets and toys and cups and clothes strewn everywhere. The kitchen sink was half filled with tepid water. There was a soggy towel and a puddle on the floor. A bottle of children's Tylenol sat open on the counter, several pills spilled. Poor Jean Philippe. He must have been frantic trying everything he could think of, awake all night. All alone.

And she slept across the hall, oblivious, useless to him, lost in her own self-pity.

Then she thought to look at the time. Three-forty-five! It wasn't even close to morning. She moved silently to tidy up the mess, draining the sink, drying the floor, picking up dishes. Her eyes scratched and drooped and her shoulders ached. She needed more sleep, even though a part of her was visualizing JP with Fifi in the waiting room of emergency, unable to rest. Surely they wouldn't make him wait too long with a limp baby in his arms. She prayed not.

Nevertheless, she couldn't stay awake, and she'd have to deal with Christian and JP's mother soon enough. So she tiptoed into the bedroom and gingerly lay down on the bed next to Christian. He stirred, rolling over and smacking her with his arm. His baby skin was so soft and warm. She caressed his arm, then reached over and stroked his back, enjoying the sturdy heat of him.

She buried her face, inhaling the scent of JP's pillow and sheets. So familiar it brought an ache to her chest and tears to her eyes. The place they'd shared such intense intimacy and passion, just forty-eight hours ago. They smelled more like a warm sweaty family, mingled with JP's wonderful man scent than they did of sex. Maybe that was her imagination running wild. Her heart thudded against her ribcage, her limbs trembling, her mind and her body flooding with memories and sensations.

That was real. That was the most real thing she'd ever experienced. With sudden clarity, Lucy realized that what she shared with Jean Philippe wasn't anything like the love she shared with Grandpa Henry.

Grandpa had always been there for her, a sheltering solid force that kept her safe and made her feel important and special through all the bumps and challenges of growing up. Which was the rightful role of a grandfather, wasn't it? He'd made it his mission to fill the gaps her parents and siblings left in her tiny, lonely childhood and done it brilliantly. She'd never once felt threatened or truly abandoned, despite the self-pity. He was a good, kind man.

But what did she give him? She let her gaze rest gently on Christian's slumbering face. Other than the sheer innocent pleasure of children. What did she know of her grandfather's life, his needs? He wouldn't have expected anything from her.

But a man had needs. Not just the physical ones, and for the first time Lucy wondered about her grandfather's personal life, since grandma had died very early. He'd spent many years alone, with only his work to occupy him, as far as she knew. Did he have lovers? Was he lonely? Was that why he had so much time for little Lucy?

Lucy's thoughts drifted to Jean Philippe. His perfect family torn apart so soon. Any dreams he may have had, for his life, for his thriving business, ripped from his chest, leaving him holding his breath, treading water, trying to make the best of a bad situation. He was every bit as good, kind and loving a man as her grandfather had been. How dare she find fault with him? What chance had she given him to adjust to her presence in his fractured life?

Perhaps he was simply grateful to have adult companionship? Undoubtedly he was enjoying the intimacy they'd shared, after nursing his dying wife, grieving her loss, and struggling alone with two young children for a year and a half. For those brief moments through the week, he could relax and let off a little steam. And what was so wrong with that? Was he even capable of giving her the focus and emotional investment she thought she needed? More importantly, could she give him what he needed?

She didn't know the answers. Lucy's eyes filled with tears, and she turned her face to the pillow to stifle the sobs that emerged from her throat. Her tears soaked into the pillow, before she finally slept, adding another layer of emotion to the tangled mess.

CHAPTER TWELVE

A VISIT to the Emergency ward could never be an easy thing, always a tug-of-war between anxiety and boredom. JP hoped a feverish two-year-old would get priority treatment. But in the middle of the night a steady stream of miserable and frantic people, punctuated by ambulances bringing more urgent cases, kept the place busy.

Fortunately, once admitted they went quickly to Pediatrics. Then JP could do nothing but stand by, chewing his lip, wringing his hands, while nurses did a series of things to his daughter. He watched as though through a tight lens, his ears ringing, his breathing shallow, feeling powerless.

Finally, a doctor showed up, but then left again too quickly. They took blood. They hydrated her and administered medication. What was happening?

JP had spent far, far too many hours in recent memory standing helplessly by a hospital bed while his beloved Fiona slowly slipped away from him. He could hardly breathe as fresh memories washed over him.

When they weren't doing something, JP just stood

beside the bed, holding his daughter's tiny hand, stroking her hot forehead, and praying. Fifi alone in a hospital bed was a terrifying sight. She was so small, so helpless. And so entirely his responsibility.

Eventually, his legs wobbly from exhaustion, he couldn't stand anymore. He dragged a chair up to the side of the bed and held onto her hand, setting his head down on the bed beside her. Nothing would happen that he wouldn't know.

He jerked awake when several women entered the room at once, blinking and staring at them in confusion. As they came into focus, he realized that one was an orderly just taking a tray away. Another was a nurse hovering and touching Fifi, measuring her temperature again. The third was a doctor come to speak to him. She looked around, saw that JP was alone.

"Mr. Roche? You're the father?"

"Yes." JP's voice cracked, and he cleared his throat and tried again. "Yes."

"Ok, we've got good news from the blood results." She said. "It's not Meningitis or any of the other more trouble-some things we routinely test for in these situations. We've given her something for the fever and her temperature has already dropped to 104. By the looks of the inflammation, it's likely an ear and throat infection, likely viral."

JP nodded.

"So we'll send you home soon. We just ask you to stick around for another hour until we can make sure her temperature is heading down toward normal range. Then she'll need a day or two of bed rest. Okay? Is your wife here?"

JP shook his head. "No wife." He swallowed.

The doctor, Doctor Singh he noted from her name tag, nodded. "I'm sorry. Are you okay? I'm sure you were anxious. The nurse will get you a blanket and pillow, and you can rest in the recliner there until we release your daughter. All right?"

"Yes. Thank you Doctor." Relief flooded JP as the doctor left. Only then did he realize the swarm of terrifying fearful thoughts that had been swimming in his mind the last few hours. Things he only vaguely recalled from reading the parenting and children's health books he'd poured over when he realized Fiona would not recover, and that he'd be alone to fend without her wise and gentle oversight.

The nurse brought him the blanket and a cup of water and he thanked her and settled into the chair after checking that Fifi was cooler and now sleeping, her breathing even and slow.

How much he wished to have Fiona here with him now? Everything, from what to make for dinner, to which brand of soap to buy, to what to do when the babies cried, was so simple for her. She always had the answers. He'd relied on her judgement. His in-laws were not wrong when they accused him of being an arms-length parent. It was partly guilt, and partly fear of screwing up, that kept him a slave to their criticism.

Not that he was careless now. He had no choice, did he? He was it. He loved his kids and would do anything for them, but he was still a man, adrift, alone, out of his depth.

Suddenly, he felt an overwhelming wish that Lucy were with him. He missed her. Her sprightly energy. Her sweetness and calm focus, those huge dark eyes that drew him in like magic and rooted him, like a deep sigh in a forest, making him feel seen and not alone. But JP couldn't substitute Lucy for Fiona just because he was alone and miserable. It had been too easy to let his imagination run wild.

He could see her as part of the family already, sharing morning coffee, playing with the kids at the beach or park, late nights cuddling while the children slept. Even folding laundry and washing dishes seemed fun and romantic when he let himself see Lucy by his side. If he were ever so lucky again, he would never take her for granted. And hadn't he said that before?

But JP couldn't indulge his idyllic daydreams. She'd clarified that was not the life she was looking for, no matter what stardust they'd shared.

He closed his eyes, recalling their last baffling exchange. She'd left him hurt and confused, reeling with a fresh sense of abandonment, shocked at how much he depended on her.

Her sudden turnaround, at first, had made him angry. She was fickle and shallow and cold-hearted. But upon further reflection, he realized she just wasn't interested in becoming a part of his complicated life. And why should she? The whole thing, with his in-laws showing up, and Christian finding her in the bathroom, must have made her uncomfortable.

She'd run away screaming, if only figuratively. She wasn't interested in his kids and all that entailed. This was one big reason he'd avoided dating in the first place, he reminded himself. He didn't want to be a burden to her. He couldn't ask her to be a part of his life. She was young and free and deserved to enjoy that.

He also couldn't risk letting her in his life. If he let them, the kids would get attached to her, more than they already were, and then when she went back to her life, they'd lose another mother figure. Fifi may not remember, but Christian certainly did. He still asked about Fiona, and he suspected he'd already taken too quickly to Lucy's gentle feminine touch. JP couldn't let that happen.

However extraordinary this tentative thing between him and Lucy had been, love was risky and unreliable. It would impede his commitment to caring for his kids. It already had. They needed stability and safety. They needed his unwavering focus.

As he drifted asleep, head lolling, he allowed himself a smidgen of self-pity. Even though on nights like tonight, he wished for and desperately needed help, he couldn't afford to worry about himself. He didn't want to, but he could do it alone.

FOR THE SECOND time in less than a week, Lucy roused from a sound sleep while in Jean Philippe's bed by a knock on his door. Her eyes shot open, her heart racing as she pieced together her current reality. No sooner had she sat up than Christian had too, bouncing to his feet.

"Papa?" He blinked in confusion at Lucy.

"Hey Christian," Lucy said. "I'm here. Your papa had to go out."

Another loud knock on the door. Christian slid from the bed and dashed off to answer it before Lucy reacted. Was he going to open the door? That wasn't okay. Her heart leapt.

"Papa!"

"No! Christian wait. You don't know who that is." She

leapt off the bed and dashed after him, arriving just as he opened the door to an older woman standing at the door surrounded by suitcases and bags. Her face lit up with a smile and Lucy's gut tugged at the resemblance to her son.

"Christian! *Mon biquet!*" She dropped her bags and crouched low to take his cheeks between her palms. "Oh, how I've missed you, Mignon." She kissed his cheeks one after the other. "Do you remember your Mamie, *mon Ange?*

Christian took a moment to process this effusive woman. Then he nodded. *"Oui, Mamie. Je me souviens."*

Huh. Lucy'd never heard Jean Philippe speaking French to Christian but he must do so sometimes.

"Excellent. Now, where is *mon bébé?*"

Lucy stepped forward and cleared her throat. "Um. Madame Roche?"

JP's mother stopped and tilted her head at Lucy.

"I'm Lucy. Jean Philippe's friend. I… uh… live across the hall." She lifted an arm to point out the open door.

Christian shuffled over to her side and tugged her pant leg, gazing up at her. "Lucy." She reached down to touch his head, but he pulled away.

"Ah, yes. He told me about you."

That stopped Lucy in her tracks. She couldn't stop the rush of heat that swept her neck and cheeks. "He did?" What had he said about her to his mother?

Madame Roche looked at her expectantly, the corners of her mouth twitching. "Is he not here?"

Christian returned, tugging again. "Lucy! Where's Papa? Where's Fifi?"

"No. I–I'm sorry." She set her hand on Christian's tousled red hair and put on her best bad-news face. "I stayed with Christian while JP took Fifi to the hospital in the middle of the night. He didn't text you?"

"Ah?" Madame Roche frowned, reached inside her purse for a cell phone and opened it. "I had it on airplane *môde* and forgot. Ah, yes I see... *oh, la. La pauvre puce.* Have you heard anything?"

Lucy shook her head, covering her mouth with her hand, whispering. "We just woke." She dashed to the bedroom for her phone and returned. "No messages."

"Lu-cy." Christian whined, pressing his face into her leg, vaguely agitated by the disruption to his routine.

She bent to pick him up and cuddle him, shocked at how much he weighed.

"Ok, then. Let's go."

"Go?"

"To the hospital, cheri. You have a car?"

"Um. Yes."

"I arrived by taxi. You shall drive."

MADAME ROCHE DID NOT CONCERN herself with the lack of car seat for Christian in Lucy's little Kia. She seemed an uncompromisingly pragmatic woman who wasted no time doubting herself. She sat in the back with Christian on her lap, the seat belt wrapped around them both. Christian had dozed off again, his head lolling back.

On the way, Madame Roche volleyed questions over the back seat. "How long have you and my son been together?"

Lucy's entire gastrointestinal system lurched. Lucy tore her gaze from the road to peer at her in the rear-view mirror and then away, thankful she had driving to occupy her and save her from the full force of Madame Roche's curiosity.

"We're not... um... together, Madame Roche–"

"Please call me Danielle. But you are, are you not? He left Christian with you, after all. He must trust you."

That gave her pause. Lucy shook her head, signalling to turn, her focus on the traffic. "No. I mean, yes, he trusts me, I suppose... but..." It seemed he did. For all that she'd felt like he'd denied her, he came to her when he needed help.

"But..." Danielle bit back her next question. "He told me about you. There was something in his voice. He seemed very intrigued. I was looking forward to meeting the new woman in his life."

"Oh." Lucy clicked her tongue. "It's complicated."

"Life is complicated, cheri."

You can say that again. "I don't think Jean Philippe is ready for anything serious, you know?"

"Is that so?"

"He said, he doesn't date, even." She cleared her throat, feeling her face heat. "JP isn't ready for another relation- ship." She stopped for a red light. "He's very protective of the kids. He's committed to caring for them, and he made a promise to F–." She glanced at Christian. "You know."

"You know about that do you?" Danielle's voice flat- tened, and Lucy detected a note of disapproval.

Lucy sighed and pulled into the visitor parking lot at the hospital.

Christian stirred. "Where're we?"

"The hospital, *ma puce*. To see Fifi."

A moment later, as Lucy turned to open her car door,

Danielle reached between the seats and gripped her arm. "Wait a moment."

Lucy turned to face her warily, her gaze darting from her piercing blue eyes, to Christian, and back again.

"He is ready."

Lucy nodded and shook her head at the same time, confused. "It hasn't been very long."

"Long enough. I think he overplays this grieving widower routine.

Lucy stared at her, speechless.

Danielle's mouth pulled in to a flat line.

Lucy swallowed, saying nothing.

"It's foolish, and those people make it worse for him, with their melodrama. They won't let him move on from Fiona."

"You think he could? That he should?" Lucy's voice rose to a squeak. She seemed unsympathetic to Jean Philippe's own loss. His grief. Their eyes caught in the mirror, Lucy frowning, and Danielle nodded brusquely.

"You think I'm cold." She pulled a face. "Pardon me for looking out for my child. He's been through a lot. My Jean Philippe is young, dynamic and virile. He needs to remarry and get on with his life. As much for his children as for himself."

Lucy gasped, glancing again at Christian, who searched out the window, frowning. She pulled her lips in and pinched her mouth closed. Was this conversation happening? This was JP's mother!

"You seem to know everything. So are you in a relationship with him or not?"

Lucy lifted a shaky hand to smooth her eyebrow, glancing down to grab her bag. "I guess we were." She glanced up and Danielle seemed to read the doubt in her eyes.

"Not anymore?"

"Where's Fifi? Where's Papa?"

"Don't misunderstand me. JP is lovely. He a wonderful man. We became good friends, very soon after we met. Instantly, really."

"Friends, eh?" She narrowed her eyes at Lucy. "Not your type?"

Lucy broke the gaze, heat flooding her face. "JP is smart, creative, kind, loving. He's fun. There's not a thing wrong with him. Someday, when he's ready, JP will make someone a lovely, amazing husband."

"But that woman is not you?"

Why did she think it should be? Was she so eager to have her son remarry that she'd settle on the first woman he met? "It's too soon, Danielle. I think you need to discuss this with Jean Phillipe." Lucy's voice came out a choked whisper. Why was she so affected by Danielle's meddling? JP could manage his own love life. He knew whether he was or was not ready.

"Are you so sure? What about you, Lucy? What do you want?"

An awkward pause stretched out as they entered the emergency ward. They arrived at the triage desk, and a nurse tilted her head at them.

After brief enquiries, the admissions nurse directed them up to the Paediatric wing. Even walking through the hospital corridors and riding up the elevator, Danielle didn't let up with the questions, though thankfully she changed the subject.

Lucy felt compelled to answer her, if only to be polite.

She chattered vaguely about her university studies and her new research job. That she was just getting started in life and hadn't thought about settling down, especially having a family.

"Mhm." Danielle approached the nursing station. The nurses were busy, and while they waited for attention, she turned her gaze back on Lucy.

Lucy swallowed, then deflected by telling her about Grandpa Henry and her special project and how she'd ended up living in her friend's studio for a few months. How she met Jean Philippe. But that her priority was her project, and she wasn't looking for a relationship, either.

"Can I help you?"

"What room are Fifi Roche and her father in please? I'm her grandmother."

The nurse consulted her computer.

Danielle watched Lucy closely. She felt compelled to continue her explanation. Though why she needed to justify herself to a stranger, she couldn't figure out.

"Room E," the nurse pointed. "End of the hall."

Danielle took a step.

Lucy gripped her arm. Dizziness and chills flooded Lucy. She couldn't walk in there and see JP after this conversation. She had to get out of here before he saw her. "Okay, it's true. We... we didn't plan on it, but we've got close. Only he doesn't want me to be a part of this... his... family," she hissed. "He said he doesn't want me spending time with his kids," she whispered.

Danielle's brow rose, and she glanced pointedly at Christian, who now rested his cheek on Lucy's shoulder, his pudgy hand gripped in her shirt. Her heart squeezed. His comfort with her belied her words.

Danielle lifted her chin and gave Lucy a smug smile, nodding, her eyes narrowed. Lucy swallowed and glanced to the floor, noting the scuff marks that peppered the shiny beige linoleum. Lucy could see how it looked, but Danielle couldn't possibly understand how complicated it was between her and JP. Danielle might want him to move on, but he wasn't ready. And in any case, he'd decided Lucy was not the woman who would change his mind.

She straightened her spine. "Okay, I admit... I have doubts. My grandfather taught me to have exceptionally high standards. I expect a man to be honourable, courageous... and loyal."

Danielle looked incredulous. "Is my son not all of these things?"

"Well, yes, but..." Lucy's face heated, and she twisted around, her gaze scanning the corridor searching for an escape route. Damn it! Her eyes burned with a flood of tears. "I feel... that, um... despite what you said, he's not ready to commit to... anyone, you know?" She sniffed, feeling a fool, and dragged the heel of her free hand across her eyes. She contradicted herself. Her emotions were all over the place.

"Where's Papa?"

Danielle reached to take Christian from her arms. "Do you think it's fair to ask him to choose between you and his motherless children?"

Lucy's stomach dropped to her shoes, leaving a hollow sick feeling. "I'm not suggesting that!" Her thoughts careened. Her face continued to flush. What was Danielle asking her?

"It could be he's just being cautious, eh? Maybe he

wants to be sure you're ready to accept him and his children. They are a package deal."

"I know that." Lucy didn't mean to snap.

Danielle's raspy voice dropped to a whisper. "Do you love him, *cheri?*"

Lucy pulled her lips between her teeth, the taste of salty tears flooding her mouth. Unformed, unclear thoughts swam in her head, shy fish in a murky tank, emerging and disappearing. One thought surfaced like a giant shark, devouring the others.

She was the foolish girl who'd fallen in love with Jean Philippe, but he didn't love her, so she had to let go. Lucy nodded involuntarily. Somehow she couldn't keep secrets from this woman, who saw her feelings as though she'd plastered them on a highway billboard. Then she shook her head, the hopelessness of her situation swamping her.

Lucy shuffled along beside Danielle who clutched her arm and propelled her down the corridor in search of Jean Philippe, following voices. The closer they got to the end of the hall, the clearer it became that Fiona's parents had beat them here.

Danielle released Lucy's arm and came to an abrupt stop in an open doorway, peering in, her face folding into a frown. Lucy peeked over her shoulder, her face tightening at the tension radiating from the room.

"It's just what we'd expect from you, John Philip." Lucy recognized Angus's slow, sad brogue. Her gaze sought him out, standing to the side. His nose was red, and his eyes moist.

Lucy's pulse kicked in revolt. Had he been crying? Had something happened to Fifi? "JP?" She pushed forward, her shoulder rubbing Danielle's.

Maeve's shrill voice picked up where Angus's drone stopped. "How could you let it get so out of hand? You should have called us sooner. What were you–?"

"Maeve." Danielle's no nonsense bark cut off Maeve's tirade.

Maeve spun to the door, her jaw dropping.

"Oh, my Lord. Danielle! Why are you here?"

"Ssshh. Calm yourself, Maeve," said Danielle. "We've just arrived. How is the child?"

Lucy picked up weird vibes from the two mother's, but her nerves were so frayed from Danielle's grilling, she couldn't focus. Maeve blocked the view beyond, but Lucy caught just enough to see that JP sprawled in a chair by the hospital bed, his long legs stretched out, his posture slumped. A thin hospital blanket drooped onto the floor. Her pulse thumped against her ribs.

Oh, no. No. She couldn't be here. How could she have slept knowing he was here alone with Fifi? How terrified he must have been. She should have supported him. But even so, she didn't belong here. Her emotions warred with each other. The urge to escape before he saw her swamped her again and she was overcome with confusion and shame.

CHAPTER THIRTEEN

"*MAMAN!*" JP stood up suddenly. "Thank God. How did you get–?"

His scowling gaze skipped over his mother's shoulder and locked on Lucy's face. "Lucy?"

She froze, the shattered expression on his face making her stomach clench and twist. With mussed hair, his beard dark, his eyes black under a lowered brow, he looked terrible, like a battle-weary soldier dragged back from the front, utterly defeated. Shell-shocked. Soul-shattered. Oh, my God!

She had to find out what happened. She pushed forward.

"Is Fifi…"

She swallowed, her throat dry as toast. Breathing was impossible. She would faint right here. As lights sparked in her peripheral vision, the thought flitted through her confused mind, at least there were medical staff nearby. Her knees wobbled.

Strong hands gripped her arms and lifted her, pressing her up against the doorjamb.

"Lucy? Why are you here?" His breath warmed her face, the familiar scent of his skin resuscitating her. The heat of his body so close penetrated her fog.

She blinked, her sight clearing.

"She drove."

JP held her up, but threw a brief glance over his shoulder at his mother, his brow furrowed. He blinked as though trying to understand a foreign language. As she gazed up into his darkened face, her chin trembled. This was all too much. "Is Fifi all right?" Her voice was tiny and tremulous, fearful.

JP's brows jerked together, his eyes flaring, and he nodded, as though just realizing that nobody knew what was going on, had perhaps assumed the worst. His Adam's apple bobbed, and he turned to face the others. "Fifi's fine. She's okay. It's a common virus. An infection."

"Oh, that's a relief," said Danielle.

"What did they say?" Maeve asked, her eyes pinched. "What caused it?"

JP shrugged and spoke through clenched teeth. "Just one of those things."

"I don't believe that for a moment," Maeve glanced at Angus for support, and back to JP. "A child doesn't get a fever like this from nothing," she spat. "It reeks of neglect."

"Maybe she picked up a bug at daycare on Friday," JP said, resigned to the flood of blame and criticism. "It happens."

Lucy couldn't stand it any more. Her body tensed and she threw off his hands. She ground her teeth and drew in a harsh breath, her lips pulled back, ready to fight, braced to defend him.

Angus sneezed into a hanky, looking up, a blush creeping over his balding forehead. He had a cold!

"Or maybe she got it from you on the weekend." The accusation was out of Lucy's mouth without planning or permission. She shoved herself away from the door, her vision coming into sharp focus. She swung her piercing gaze from the befuddled man blowing his nose to his shrew of a wife and back again, noting odd details, like the fact she liked the pretty green beads that Maeve's reading glasses dangled from, and that Angus had a coffee stain on the front of his blue shirt, as though time had slowed to a crawl. "Why are you so determined to find fault with Jean Philippe?"

Maeve bristled, her shoulders rising to her ears as the corners of her mouth creased, and Angus looked on, his neck disappearing into his shirt collar. She was the woman, that if she were your professor, or your boss, you would hide from.

JP reached out to set a steadying hand on her arm, and she flinched away, too agitated to accept the gesture. She wasn't finished. "He's a good father. He's loving and atten-tive, and he's done nothing but sacrifice his own needs for his children, as he did for your daughter. Why can't you accept that it's not his fault Fiona died!"

Danielle's face froze in rictus of a smile, equal parts shock and delight. Well, what did it matter? Someone had to speak up. She was expendable. A red shirt that didn't belong here, anyway. It might as well be her.

A keening moan escaped from Maeve, as she covered her mouth with one hand, and reached back to clutch at

Angus's sleeve with the other. "How can she say that? Who do you think you are, young lady?"

"Me?" Lucy wavered. Who was she? Why was she here? What was her place in this family drama? She shook her head. She scoffed. "Nobody."

Jean Philippe said nothing, keeping his gaze locked on the floor. Oh, God, what had she done? Her outburst embarrassed him. He'd be furious.

Danielle reached out to place a solid hand on Lucy's shoulder, but she was already twisting away, leaning out the door, jerking like a kite being tugged by a gust of wind. She had to get out of here. Now!

Not ten steps down the hall, strong, familiar hands grabbed her from behind. She spun to face Jean Philippe, her gaze lifting to meet his. He faltered, and she could well imagine that he didn't know what to say to her. She saw nothing but pain and regret in his tired eyes.

"Thank you." His voice cracked, rusty from sleep and fatigue.

She nodded, jerking one shoulder in a half shrug. Even when she'd behaved atrociously, he maintained good manners. He was gentle and kind down to the soles of his feet, and her heart lurched in pain at his goodness, and what she had grazed with the tips of her fingers but could not hold on to. He likely felt he had to thank her for watching Christian. They were the last words he'd ever speak to her.

She pulled away, the doubts and insecurities surging in. "It's the least I could do after all your help... with my project."

He searched her eyes with his piercing blue gaze, as though tracing her features, filing them away.

She averted her gaze and shuffled back another step.

He reached up and rubbed the back of his neck, cleared his throat and tilted his head to the side as though it were stiff, dropping his intense gaze to her chin. "We're checking out of here soon. But we're okay coming home in a taxi."

Right. She got it. He didn't have his car, but he didn't need her anymore. He didn't want her here, with his family. She need not get involved in his private affairs any longer. "Okay," she said with a feeble laugh. Her stomach convulsed and her smile felt brittle. She couldn't look up, and hated her weakness, but her eyes stung. She had to escape.

He stepped closer and set his hand on her arm again. "I'm sure you want to head home and... get some work done?" He was trying to be diplomatic, but it was obvious. She was in the way. He'd dismissed her.

"Mhm. Yup. I do," she said, her voice watery.

"Okay, I'll... uh, see you later?"

The elevator dinged its arrival, like Tardis come to whisk her away to another dimension just in time.

"Sure." Lucy pulled out of his grasp and turned, stepping through the open doors. She let the doors slide closed without turning around, tears already spilling their boundaries.

JP's HEAD ACHED, his hands shook and his eyes drooped. He might have been caught in an Akkers gravity net, every effort to lift his weary tentacles overwhelmed by the cosmic force of his captivity. He pinched the bridge of his nose trying to focus his vision. Mama set her hand on his arm and looked up at him. Just having her here brought him immeasurable comfort, wrapping him in a patchwork quilt of reassurance, bringing with her generations of wisdom and experience that soothed him. He could feel the adrenaline of the past hours draining away like the last grains of sand through an hourglass, leaving him empty, transparent and fragile.

"Lie down with Fifi. Try to get some sleep."

He nodded, as mute as his sleeping daughter.

"Christian and I will have a visit. Isn't that right, ma puce? Shall we have some breakfast? And then you can show Mamie all the new toys you got since I last saw you, eh?" She tousled his tangled russet head and led him to the kitchen.

Jean Philippe had no energy to argue. This was the difference between his in-laws and his mother. They piled on abuse, she cocooned him in unconditional love. She knew how hard he tried, how much he gave, and worried about him overdoing it, all alone. He was so very tired of being alone.

He crawled into bed so as not to disturb Fifi. His gazed danced over the fine strands of dark hair pasted to her pale forehead, the blue veins that shone through her transparent eyelids, fragile and peaceful. He filled his lungs and let go a long drawn-out sigh of relief. She slept without thrashing now, and probably would for the next day as she recovered from her fever and infection. He'd only have to wake her to administer her next dose of antibiotic and hoped she did sleep for hours.

Laying his head down into the indentation in his pillow, he caught a whiff of something odd that detonated a roaring rumble through his tired blood, a freight train of sensation that shoved his tired heart up against the cage of his ribs with a whoosh. A scent so soft, sweet and feminine, so familiar, it hurt, his body reacting before his brain caught up. His pulse pounded, and his fingers, toes and lips tingled anticipating reward. It shook every thought from his head and left him dazed.

Lucy.

She'd lain here, next to Christian just a few hours ago. JP closed his eyes, pressed his face into the pillow, digging his fingers into the creased sheets, inhaling and letting her scent wash over him and fill up his senses. His dick jerked in sudden anticipation, and he let the sensation rush by, riding it like a magic carpet, letting it trigger memories... images, sounds and tastes of Lucy and losing himself in them like a man immersing himself in a bottle of whiskey, welcoming the blur of reality, knowing full well how he'd suffer in the morning, and yet unable to stop himself.

His time with Lucy had been brief, too brief, but it had filled him up. She'd made him feel alive for the first time in years. He couldn't give her up. He wanted more.

Jean Philippe wanted her. He wanted her body next to his, entwined, shuddering, panting with need. His dick hailed him again and his hips rolled off the bed in involuntary greeting to her ghostly limbs wrapping his torso, the memory of her weight on him. But he also wanted the playful build up of their banter and flirtation, her sweet touches and the look of hunger in her wide dark eyes that transformed her from pixie into vixen.

He also craved the mellow erasure of separateness that cocooned them afterwards, when they became one body, one mind, one heart thumping out the rhythm of their synchronized heartbeat tumbling back down from the heavens.

That feeling, of belonging, of bonding and trust and partnership. He needed that, and he thought he and Lucy had crossed a secret boundary into that sacred shared space.

Now he didn't know what to do. There was no clear path forward. She didn't want him. He was a selfish bastard. What would Fiona think now? His resolve hadn't lasted two years. He'd crumbled under the weight of responsibility. The promise he'd made on her deathbed felt like an un-winnable battle.

His chest squeezed, the thought Lucy might be lost to him a giant boa constrictor slowly tightening around his chest, his breathing stopping in its path until his temples throbbed and he saw shooting stars in the blackness behind his closed lids. The emptiness of space would be a welcome respite.

It couldn't be. It couldn't be.

Despite his fatigue, he couldn't fall asleep. JP's mind cycled through the last twelve hours, replaying like an infinite video loop, each singular moment stabbing his heart, making it bleed a little more.

His panic rising degree by degree along with Fifi's temperature.

His sense of desperate isolation.

Realizing he had to get her to the hospital.

Reaching out for Lucy's help without hesitation. He needed her. But he knew she'd pulled away. Cut him off. She owed him nothing. Particularly regarding his kids.

But this was an emergency.

That made it okay, didn't it? Trying not to impose on

Lucy, he'd called Brian for a ride, and then realized he didn't want to wake Christian and drag him along. He'd be cranky and demanding, and JP needed to focus on Fifi. He'd been so frantic, he'd barely registered her reaction. Had she minded? Was she annoyed? What did she think of him?

Later, everything blurred. He hadn't been asleep long when Maeve and Angus burst in, primed for battle. He'd sent them a quick text in the early morning. It hadn't occurred to him to call them in the middle of the night. But he hadn't needed their hysterics, anyway. His own hysteria was sufficient.

This emergency was just the crisis they'd been waiting for. So even though he knew to expect it, his brain was barely functional when they'd arrived and lit into him as usual. Too tired and numb to even feel his usual irritation and frustration, let alone respond, he wanted to lie down like the beaten dog he was and let them beat him.

Everything afterwards unfolded in slow motion.

His mother walked in.

Right behind her, Lucy. Lucy!

He hadn't expected to see her amid his family crisis. He was incapable of processing his feelings then. His heart beat in his chest in a slow steady boom of thunder like a timpani drum, drowning out their voices. A bubble of fatigue and shock surrounded him and muffled sound, slowing time. He couldn't even speak.

And then she rose, righteous and indignant, like Joan of Arc, to defend him, and to challenge Maeve and Angus. Even in his numbed state, seeing how they cowered in the face of her wrath was impressive, but out of habit, guilt consumed and moved him to soothe their frayed emotions.

Why did she do that? What did that mean? Was she a champion of underdogs, as though that weren't kick ass enough? Or was she just fed up with his willingness to tolerate their abuse?

Did she pity him? Or perhaps there was some residual tenderness, remaining from their sweet loving time together. Had she reacted without thinking, and then realizing she was acting out a role she didn't want, turned on her heel and fled? She couldn't escape fast enough, that was clear. And JP knew he had no right to ask her to stay, no matter how much he might want to keep her close.

His mind full of images of Lucy, dressed in armour, astride a white horse, sword swinging, the champion of his salvation, mythical and out of reach, did his body succumb to the supernatural power of the dragnet of fatigue and he slipped into a deep hypnotic sleep.

"JEAN PHILIPPE. MON ANGE. SE RÉVEILLER."

He awoke with a start to Mama jostling his arm. "Hm?"

"Wake up now, Cher. It's getting late. The children want you. And we're going to eat dinner."

"Dinner?" He jackknifed up, grappling to find his bearings. "Time s'it?" He'd been dreaming of Lucy, holding her in his arms, looking down into her sweet smiling face, his own face stretching in response, happiness filling him like an airship. The bubble of happiness popped as reality settled on him with a thump that knocked the breath from his lungs. The dream was false. She might be his heroic fantasy, but in the real world she didn't want him and his messy life. He checked the bed beside him. "Where's Fifi?"

"It's late afternoon. Fifi needs her medicine."

JP's heart slammed to his throat. "I missed it!"

"Non, non. I gave her one at about eleven. It's time for the next already. But she wants you. And I need your help to feed her."

"Why didn't you wake me sooner?"

"You were dead to the world, so I let you sleep." She tilted her head, studying him with a knowing maternal half smile. "You're so busy taking care of everyone, you need someone to take care of you. But... I knew you'd want to see how she is doing."

"Yes, of course." Achy and bleary-eyed, he staggered to the bathroom to splash cold water on his face. He could have slept through the night. But Mama knew better than to let him. "*Merci.*" He took the sippy-cup of juice and dropper of medicine Mama handed him. Thank God she was here to help out. He would have been miserable in this situation without her.

Fifi sat in front of the TV watching dancing dragons, wrapped up like a *pain au chocolat* in her favourite fuzzy blanket. Christian played doctor, his toy stethoscope around his neck, ministering to her. A watery smile pulled at JP's face. They were so cute. Pressure built under his diaphragm, his breath accelerating as his body purged the last of the toxic stress. His eyes welled with tears of relief, and his chin quivered. His little girl was back.

"*Maman.* Did you check her temperature?"

"Almost normal," she called from the kitchen where she was banging pots and dishes around. "She's bounced right back."

He sent up a silent prayer of thanks, putting to bed the myriad fears and horrors that always hovered on the dark margins of a parent's consciousness. He went to Fifi, sat on the floor next to her and gave her a big kiss, *Mwah, mmmwah*, while feeling the relative coolness of her brow with his lips. "Ah, my little Fifi, darling. Open wide, love." Absently, she gripped his fingers with her little hand as he squirted the syrup into her mouth, but kept her eyes on the television, calm and content. He handed her the juice, and she released him to grip it with both hands.

Christian said, "Don't worry Papa. I'm doctoring Fifi for you. You can sleep s'more."

JP bent to kiss the top of Christian's head. "Thank you, Christian. You're an excellent doctor." He straightened. "In that case, I'm going to go have a quick shower. I stink."

A FEW MINUTES LATER, stripped bare and scrubbing himself in a hot shower, another wave of visceral memories flowed over him along with the sluice of soap suds, shampoo and hot water. He looked at his own hand, splayed against the wall tiles, and his muscles tensed with remembered desire, his dick lighting up like the Doctor's sonic screwdriver. He groaned.

Lucy.

They'd shared a few steamy Saturday nights in here together, too. Including, he could never forget, the last one, their transcendent night of intense pleasure and sweet, almost painfully sweet coupling. Closing his eyes, he saw the look in Lucy's eyes, dark and deep as a bottomless pool he wanted to sink into, knowing the water was warm and sweet, and would surround him and keep him buoyant like a balm.

A fist of truth punched him in the gut, knocking the wind out of him. If he hadn't already known he'd fallen for Lucy, he couldn't deny it after that night. He loved her.

And the awkward morning that followed. The end. Was it?

He must be whacked. He couldn't seem to hold back the hot tears that leaked out between his eyelids and thickened his throat.

Luuuuu-cy. He set his forehead against the tile wall and pounded it with the back of his fist. One, two, three.

He bowed his head under the stream of water, his eyes closed, reliving that morning. What the hell had happened? Just when he'd finally admitted to himself that he wanted her in his life. Just when he was on the cusp of acknowledging that he'd fallen for her, she'd pulled away. How had their world disintegrated so suddenly, like a sand castle torn apart by a crashing wave?

Why wouldn't she talk to him?

He towelled himself dry and tugged on some soft sweats and a t-shirt, shaky and low-spirited.

CHAPTER FOURTEEN

THE SILENCE from Studio 7D was deafening, pulsing like an ECG graph, measuring out the slow sad beats of her dying heart. Was hers the only one that was bleeding out from the wound of his absence? Had his line gone flat? Did he not feel it?

It demanded all of Lucy's focus and discipline to ignore it. She marched, sidled and shuffled to her door numerous times throughout the day, resolved to cross the hall and at least ask how Fifi was doing, only to drag herself back to her computer, dejected and confused. She hadn't known what to expect after the encounter at the hospital. Jean Philippe had said he'd 'see her later.' But the entire day had passed and... nothing.

He hadn't meant it. He was only being polite. Lucy recognized that her being there had freaked him out, and he was eager for her to leave. Her cheeks still burned when she remembered her outburst. How embarrassed JP must be by this strange woman screeching at his in-laws all the time. He'd told her why he went easy on them, but she couldn't listen. He was furious with her. Fed up and finished. Another example of a budding romance that fizzled like water on a hot rock, leaving nothing but a puff of hot air in its wake. But it felt different.

So why did she expect him to come knocking on her door? She tried to reconcile the sense her head talked with the longings of her heart. She might wish to go back to the easy friendship and blissful connection of their few weeks together, before reality crashed in. Why wouldn't she? She had never been so compatible and connected as she had with Jean Philippe. Never. If she knew that kind of bond was even possible, she might have been looking for it, the way Anna did.

But Jean Philippe knew. He'd lost the love of his life. To him Lucy was nothing but a diversion from his lonely existence. She'd got it all wrong.

Her romantic dream was unrealistic. It didn't fit with his wishes or his needs, and it wasn't part of Lucy's plan either.

Time to grow up, steel her ovaries, and direct her thoughts toward her own, genuine goals. Her own life.

A mere two months ago, the desire to vindicate and celebrate Grandpa Henry's legacy and put the usurper Peter Sinnehausser in his place had consumed her. The opportunity to pursue that dream had made her ecstatic. Many people put their faith in her ability to do this. Though her family were dubious and somewhat indifferent, her employer, most coworkers and friends were behind her. Everyone had helped make it possible by committing to cover her projects in her absence, hold her position, and make available the use of this studio without cost. She owed it to them, and she owed it to herself to follow through with her promise. Most of all, she owed it to Grandpa Henry to accomplish what she'd set out to do. She couldn't bear to see the brilliant man's life's work slip into oblivion.

She checked her email in-box first, sending quick updates to friends and colleagues. There was a short message from Mom, in Amsterdam at a conference, asking how she was making out and when she'd be back to 'normal.'

Lucy took a deep breath and let out a long sigh. At least they hadn't forgotten she'd existed. Whatever. She wasn't doing it for them.

As she scrolled through her website, her heart swelled in her chest. With pride at what she'd accomplished so far, but also with boundless gratitude for JP's contribution. She still had a good chunk of research papers to sift through, but she'd caught up with inputting all her notes from Grandpa's journals as well as completed the chronology of key events in his life, both professional and personal.

The framework JP had created for her worked beautifully, and with his help she knew enough to tweak a few things to suit her needs. Not only did it simplify entering new facts, but it gave her ample opportunity to expand and enrich the story with family photos and personal anecdotes. And it looked fantastic. What would she have done without JP's talent and ideas?

Lucy had no experience with web design. This presentation, an easy way to share her work, wouldn't have occurred to her, let alone been possible, without his help. She was a dry academic researcher, without JP's ability to engage and entertain with shape, proportion, colour.

As a psychologist, she'd studied a little about media, its

forms and the way it connected with the human brain. She'd taken one course on advertising years ago. So she understood what he was doing, but his facility and mastery, and that he made communication aesthetically pleasing and easy to navigate were mysteries to her. No wonder gold seals and accolades decorated those framed ads on his wall. He was really good.

Last week, she'd made the website live, with only a landing page and the menu. Now, satisfied with her work, she was ready to make it public. With a trembling hand and a sick stomach, she hit publish on the remaining pages. Recalling JP's instructions, she checked to see it loaded properly, then sat scrolling through her creation, wondering what kind of reception it would get from Grandpa's colleagues and her own. Finally, she sent the prepared group email with a link inviting the most important people in his field to look at it.

LUCY LET OUT her breath on a long sigh.

Instead of the excitement she'd expected to feel, her shoulders slumped, something in her chest pinching with regret. This is what she'd planned and worked for. This was moment her work over the past two months culminated. But she didn't experience the thrill she'd anticipated this moment would bring. In fact, she felt flat.

After his help, their shared work on its design, and how much she cared for him, she'd wanted to share this moment with Jean Philippe. He would already have subscribed to the page, so he might notice it was live if he wasn't too busy, but would he even care? She used to think achieving this goal would bring her so much joy and satisfaction. But now the only thing she felt was an aching sense she wanted something more.

She was proud of her accomplishment, but wanted to share it with someone special. Grandpa was gone, and now so was JP.

Not for the first time, she thought about all he'd given up to care for his children alone. He was a brilliant designer. All those awards proved that's what he should do, not design websites and logos for small businesses while working from home. It was a waste of his talent. Yet he'd given it all up.

She recalled her conversation with Anna.

What would Grandpa Henry think of JP now, if he met him? The interview played out in her mind. She'd be upstairs, putting on her last coat of mascara, and Grandpa would invite JP into the living room to sit down. JP would shake his hand, and Grandpa would lower himself back into his favourite armchair, his books and papers piled up beside it, pull off his reading glasses and level a gaze at JP, intending to scrutinize, perhaps designed to intimidate.

She laughed a little, she could see it.

JP would sit down opposite, his posture relaxed and confident, and his face would open with that gorgeous white smile, his warmth, intelligence and confidence shining through.

Such confidence in a young man would impress Grandpa, but he wouldn't show it, leaning back and narrowing his wrinkled old sea green gaze at him, waiting a beat or two to see if he squirmed.

Lucy knew this because she'd spied on a few of these

interviews, peering around corners. She'd watched a few guys squirm.

She frowned now. Did he want her to grow up lonely, with only him for company?

Lucy had never questioned his motives. Grandpa was always right. He always knew more and stayed one step ahead of everyone else. He always had her best interests at heart, didn't he? When she was alone, he filled the void with reading and games and adventures and gentle, nurturing conversation.

What exactly had he been doing all those years?

She thought about what a timid, cowering little girl she'd been, always dismissed and shunted to the side, a sweet fragile shell of a child her parents and older siblings loved in some abstract way, like a hollow porcelain doll, but never really took the time to know. Or just didn't get, the way Grandpa did. No one wanted to hurt her, but Grandpa wanted more for her.

Or…

A little fizzy bubble of some confusing emotion puffed inside Lucy's chest, and grew and grew, filling her up from the inside with lightness until she could almost feel herself lifting up out of her chair, a helium filled Lucy-shaped balloon, her feet leaving the floor. Was it hope? Pride? Confidence? A bit of all three, perhaps?

Maybe he wanted more from her.

Grandpa Henry wasn't trying to set the bar so impossibly high for anyone Lucy might want to love. But he knew how hungry for love and acceptance that neglected girl was and wanted to make sure she didn't settle just to fill that void. Rather, he wanted to make sure she knew and loved herself before deciding someone or something outside herself could ever be the sole source of her happiness.

Was JP that for her? No!

A puff of gratitude joined the gassy mixture of emotions that lifted her up.

She didn't love JP because of what he did or could do for her. Nor because of some external expectation that she should want or need a life partner to complete her. But she did love him, from her heart, knowing what was important to her, what she wanted, and what she could offer. And that this was the right thing.

She simply loved him, and knew that they had something special together, and that she had something of value to contribute to their partnership. And also that JP saw and valued her. Love from a position of strength and self-knowledge. This was Grandpa's true legacy.

CHAPTER FIFTEEN

THE TABLE SET, his children already seated around it, their faces scrubbed clean. He sighed. Mama made it look too easy. Sure she'd raised his brother and himself, but still. It wasn't fair. He glanced up to meet her smiling gaze, and understanding shone from her eyes like a benediction. She understood.

He shook his head and sent her a grateful smile.

"Sit down." With no need to ask, she set a glass of red wine in front of him.

He grunted, the air leaving his lungs in a short burst, his gratitude so complete. He took a gulp of the wine, sitting back, letting his guard down for once.

After serving the kids, Mama set a plate of food in front of him, but he poked at it, barely registering what it was. He had no appetite. He occupied himself more with helping Fifi eat hers, watching with pride and satisfaction as she tried to feed herself, relieved that her appetite and energy were back.

Christian seemed to sense his usual chatter would be too much, or maybe all the stress of the trip to the hospital had overwhelmed and tired him, too.

Despite his long sleep and shower, JP felt a heaviness in his bones, an ache in his chest that wouldn't let up, that wouldn't let him take a full lungful of air. His eyes and throat felt scratchy, and he thought maybe it was his turn to have a bout of the virus that had affected Fifi, and Angus.

Or if he were honest with himself, maybe it was because his thoughts dwelled on Lucy, tossing in his head like debris in a storm.

The urge to do something, anything, to turn things around, to go back to the way they were–that bright effervescent moment that had caught them up and ended so soon–would not cease to agitate and shove at him like a bully in a bar, even though he knew it was hopeless and he had no fight left in him.

A long sigh escaped from deep in his chest.

How many times must he tell himself that she didn't want what he offered? It didn't matter he might want her in his life. She'd left no doubt in his mind she wanted distance from his kids, his in-laws, his compromises, his heavy burden.

Hadn't she?

Even if she hadn't pushed him away, he knew it was the right thing to let her go. He'd already leaned too hard on her, just because it was such a huge relief to have a caring friend, someone close he could call on when he felt lonely. She had her own goals, her own life, unencumbered and full of promise. He'd be doing her no favours by insinuating his chaotic life into hers. She'd only saved him from having to make that decision.

"Are you feeling yourself yet?"

The dirty dishes lay untouched on the table. Christian slipped out of his chair and made his way to the living room. JP unclipped Fifi from her chair and she went to her Mamie's lap for a cuddle. He glanced up at Maman, who sat still with her arms around Fifi, her hands folded, fingers interlaced, observing him.

JP knew that expression well. When their gazes caught, she narrowed her eyes and dipped her chin in the way she always had when he'd been at home, as though she were waiting for him to acknowledge some wrongdoing. She had some sixth sight so he could keep no secrets from her, and she could see right into his head and heart with that maternal laser vision.

His eyes widened then slid away from her, the old flight or fight rush of adrenaline pulsing out from his chest, liquifying his gut. He felt sweat blossom and swallowed, his throat dry. She still had that effect on his lizard brain. The urge to confess bubbled up so he could get it over with and go to his room. Except he didn't know what he'd done wrong.

"*Maman!*" His confusion must have shown on his face because Maman clicked her tongue, sighed, lifted her eyes to God. She set Fifi down as she stood up to clear the table.

"Seriously, *mon biquet*? You don't understand?"

JP pursed his lips, twisting his mouth to the side, nibbling on the inside of his cheek. He felt trapped. He blinked at her. Was this about Lucy? Had she indeed read his mind?

She returned from whisking the dishes into the sink and folded her arms across her chest, and he blinked at her again, turning his head to the side, but keeping his eyes on her patient but still expectant expression. "What are you going to do about that girl?"

He pushed his jaw forward. "What can I do? She doesn't want... this."

"Did she say that? Hasn't she shown you how she feels?"

"Not... no, but, she made it clear what she wants."

"Have you also? Made told her how you feel?"

His shoulders jerked up. Had he? No, he hadn't. "I..." He broke off, unsure, and the skin around Mama's eyes tightened with the beginnings of a smile and with renewed clarity he lifted his chin and shook his head, his throat tightening. "How can I ask for what I want, *Maman*? I don't dare tempt fate again."

She huffed. "You always were a lucky boy."

He knew what she meant, but he didn't feel lucky.

She reached forward to cover his hand with hers, squeezing. "You were given beauty, intelligence and strength. You have talent and knew what you wanted to do with it, so have always been able to earn a good living. I never worried about you." She tilted her head, her mouth pulling into a line, as though his endless good luck left her baffled. She cupped his scuffed cheek in one palm. "You met a beautiful woman in college and, voila! she fell in love with you, agreed to marry you, and gave you two delightful, healthy children."

As she spoke, he let memories of his easy, blessed life flit through his mind. She was right. He felt a familiar wave of guilt trickle through him, that his life had been so easy.

The problem was, she was right. He didn't deserve another chance. He'd had the perfect life. The perfect wife. And he took her for granted. He took all that happiness without paying. No one deserves that much happiness. The heaviness descended again. "And then she died and left me alone. Now it's payback time."

"Life, *mon chou*, is not always sweet, but neither is it vindictive. It cannot be an unbroken chain of pearls. Without valleys, we wouldn't know hills. Without darkness, we wouldn't recognize the light for what it is."

He knew this. "Are you saying because I was blessed with good fortune, I deserved to lose the love of my life?"

"No one deserves misfortune. Yet it comes. But the rest of your life lies ahead. Who said you're only given one shot at happiness, and when it's gone, that's all you get? You must make of your life what you can, at every turn."

He averted his gaze from her face, his jaw tense, his teeth gnashing. A small, tight seed of hope sprouted some place deep inside him, pressing up, pulsing with potential life, and he pushed it back down, knowing he could never let it bloom. The disappointment would be too great to bear.

"Is this what Fiona wanted for you?"

"I promised her..." His voice went watery and his throat narrowed, choking off his words. He tried again. Pushing through the tension that twisted his brow and curled his lips into a grimace, he stressed. "I. Promised. Her."

"What did you promise her?"

That I wouldn't be selfish! "To always put the children first. Not to get caught up in my life and offload their care to... to Maeve, or you, or anyone!"

"And have you done that?"

He rose, agitated and swung his arms. "Of course not! You know that!"

"Shh. Shh. You'll upset the children."

He heaved a sigh, sat again and rested his head on his hands, gripping his hair, digging the heels of his hands into his eye sockets. He hadn't done it, yet, but would he? Especially if he were tired, overwhelmed or an opportunity for pleasure came along. Or worse yet, a loving, nurturing woman who wanted to ease the load from his shoulders. Did he trust himself to never do that again?

Mama laughed, the sound puffing through her nose, something about the sound making him feel like a child again, insecure and awash in self-doubt, despite all his good fortune. "You're still lucky, Jean Philippe. Here you are, tucked away, with your business and your children."

She paused, and he lowered his hands to the table and set his head on them.

"You're a good man, *mon fils*. Here you stay, seeing no one. You don't even date. And yet another chance at love has come knocking on your door. Another great gift awaits you."

Was she referring to Lucy? Lucy was a gift?

"The true measure of a man's character is how he deals with adversity, non? Does he wallow in self-pity, cursing God? Does he give up and lie down, or pick himself up and start again?"

He looked up, a plume of awareness rising from his gut, his entire body flooding with heat. The shoot of hope raised its small green head, searching for light.

"This is your life, *mon biquet*. What are you going to do about it?"

The shoot stretched, pushing its face to the sky, the weight of the dark soil crumbling away, filling his chest with an unfurling sensation. He knew what he would do about it, the jolt of effervescent life making his heart lighter and his limbs tingle.

CHAPTER SIXTEEN

A SUDDEN BOLD knock on her door jolted Lucy from her deep thoughts.

Before she rose from her chair, her body knew it was him. Her heart pummelled her ribcage like a wild beast crashing to get out, sending adrenaline-rich blood rushing to her head, neck, and chest.

She stepped forward on shaky legs and peeked. She jerked away from the door. It was him! Her stomach clenched and rolled over, the press of bile making her suddenly nauseous. Stepping back, she reached for the handle, her hand trembling.

He knocked again.

She threw open the door. There he was.

He was panting, breathless, as though he'd just run up the stairs and she glanced down the corridor, confused. Opposite, his studio door stood ajar, the tinny sound of the television carried out with the faintest scents of dish soap, chicken, lemons. Her own harsh breathing echoed loudly in her ears.

When she saw his face, a fifty-car pile up crashed in her chest while her heart was a semi-tractor trailer jack-knifed in her throat. Their gazes locked for a terrifying moment. She very nearly fell into his arms, the urge to be held by him almost overwhelming, yet she held back, rigid. He'd come to feel like family to her, like home, the way Grandpa Henry's embrace had always been the safe and loving place she knew she would be okay. But that wasn't true. Why was he here?

"Jean Philippe!"

His gaze caught hers, focussed and intent, and his chest lifted with a huge breath. "Lucy."

She stumbled backwards. Sudden fear turned her stomach to stone, exploding out through her limbs in spasms, goosebumps cascading up her arms and neck, down her spine. She was sweating like she'd just done a two hour power yoga class.

"Is Fifi alright?" Lucy's voice emerged as a tremulous whisper, her eyes drinking in the sight of him. He nodded silently, his darkly shadowed jaw, his earnest blue eyes that scanned her face, studied her lips. He was here for another reason then. She lifted sweaty palms to her hot cheeks, pressing to contain the wide smile of welcome that pulled at her face at his presence. Pressing to ease the sensations gathering into a storm inside her.

"I understand if you don't want to talk to me. I'm sorry," he said.

"What are you sorry for?" She gestured for him to enter her studio and followed him in. "It's me that made an ass of myself and yelled at your in-laws. Again. I thought you were finished with me."

He stopped and spun to face her. "What? No!"

"You're not… mad?"

JP dipped his chin and tilted his head slightly, taking her upper arms gently in his palms, sending hot and cold shivers through her, as though the semi had spilled some hot combustible mix. His voice soothed her fears. "Of course not. You're my champion. My hero." A flush climbed his dark stubbled jaw, each angle and indent familiar and well-loved.

His nervous chuckle confused her, and she stayed silent. His hero?

JP's eyes softened, sending heat ricocheting through her bloodstream. "You really are, you know, in more ways than one." He lifted a hand and stroked her cheek with his knuckle, sending shivers galloping over her skin, raising goosebumps.

Lucy still could think of no reply. She didn't understand what he was trying to say. Her head shook once.

"You saved me, Lucy." He chuckled. "And not just from my in-laws." He sobered. "From myself."

Lucy frowned, and he leaned in.

His eyes sparkled like moonstones, intense, clear, focussed and she felt a tightness in her chest. Felt her breath stall. JP lifted a hand, palm up, and she had the weird sense that he was offering her some treasure. As though his heart, open and vulnerable rested there, and her own heartbeat accelerated while her thoughts swirled, trying to make sense of the possibilities. He patiently waited for her to say something. Do something. But what?

"I… I don't understand."

JP considered her for another breath or two, then dropped his hands, running one through his hair, angling to the side, revealing his own nerves. "I've had time to reconsider. Or rather *Maman* has thankfully given me the smack on the head I needed." He looked back, his eyes locked on hers again. "I've been a fool, Lucy."

Lucy's mouth went dry. She was as much afraid of as thrilled by what he'd say next.

"I didn't think I was ready for this. I thought I had to do this alone, or I'd be betraying Fiona and somehow abandoning my commitments. But since I met you, everything's changed. I feel lighter. I feel alive again." He swallowed. When he stepped closer to her, she felt dizziness wash over her. He reached forward and took her hand lightly in his, lifting it up, and she looked at their interlaced fingers, her heart tripping.

"Lucy, I've fallen in love with you." His thumb caressed the back of her hand. "I didn't plan it. I wasn't looking for it. I actually thought it never could happen again. But there you were. Here you are."

"But… your kids. You said you don't want–"

He stopped her with a fingertip over her lips. "I'm sorry I was cowardly and tried to push you away. I don't think I told you what I really want, Lucy."

She waited, her heart thumping in her chest, pumping blood up into her head like a thermometer on a hot summer day, temperature rising, higher and higher. Her legs felt weak and wobbly as she focussed on the tiny beads of sweat that bloomed on his brow.

"Let me make it perfectly clear. I want you. If you'll have me. Us." He flashed a shy smile.

Joyful tears spilled from her eyes, and her face stretched into a wide smile as her chest filled with a bubble of air. Her chin wobbled, and she tried to pull her lips in to stop their trembling. His mouth tugged to one side in a flashing grin and he bent to drop a kiss on her slobbery lips.

He nodded. "Yes. I have kids that make my life messy and complicated." His smile was sweet and apologetic. "Yes, I have in-laws." And he sobered. "Yes, there's a ghost in my family. Can you love a man who comes with a pile of baggage? Can you give us a chance?"

She shook her head, her voice gurgling with tears. "Not baggage. A treasure trove of riches. A life that will never be dull." She smiled through her tears.

He pulled her to him, cupped her face between his palms, and swiped the tears from her cheeks with his thumbs. Then Jean Philippe bent and dropped butterfly kisses on her cheeks, her eyes, and finally her mouth. Every cell in her body reached up to meet him, her heart swelling with love for him.

"I love you, Jean Philippe. You are the most amazing, wonderful man I've ever known."

He pulled away an inch and whispered, "As good a man as Grandpa Henry?"

She nodded, her cheeks thrilling at the gentle caress of his palms, holding her as though he thought he held the precious gemstone, yet not tightly, and he slid his hands around to the back of her head to nest it as she looked up at him, her eyes soaking in the beautiful sight of him looking back at her. She saw in his blue, blue eyes the naked truth. "Even better, because you're mine. I think you're exactly what Grandpa had in mind for me."

"Is this what you want? I didn't think this is the life you were looking for either."

Her shoulders came up to her ears and she tilted her

head to one side. "Life is what you make of it. Let's find out together."

"Will you walk with me?" His hand slid down her arm and he tugged on her fingers. "Come?"

She hesitated. "Isn't your mom still there with the kids?"

"She's expecting you." He grinned. "Come home with me, Lucy."

Lucy's mouth fell open and she shook her head in bewilderment, letting him pull her slowly across the hall, through his open door.

Christian looked up from a mess of paper and art supplies on the floor. "Lucy! See what I did!" He stood up and strode toward her on his sturdy legs with a sheet of stiff paper in his hand. "I made a fambly picture."

Lucy released JP's hand and took a tentative step toward Christian, squatting and taking his picture. A crowd of bold blob people with various too-large misshapen heads clustered in the centre, brightly filled in with blotches of marker and crayon in blue and orange. Almost like a Matisse, she thought. Though childish, she could see he already had his father's talented eye for composition and colour. "It's wonderful, Christian. You really are an artist!"

"It's Papa, Fifi an' me." Christian pointed them out with chubby stained fingers. "An' there's Mamie. An' Mama. And Gran'ma and Grandpa." That explained the extra figures in the group, one of them sweetly and tragically inside a rectangle. "An' this is you, Lucy." He put his smudged finger on another figure, with a smaller head crowned with large spiked hair, and looked up at her, his blue eyes earnest and proud.

Fifi toddled up to them, setting her hand on Lucy's thigh to steady herself. "Yoofy," she said.

"Fifi?" Jean Philippe's breathless voice was incredulous and joyful. "What did you say, darling?"

Fifi lifted her blue gaze to her father and spoke again, patting Lucy's thigh with her little pudgy hand, insistent. "Yoofy!"

Danielle, standing by the kitchen bar with a tea towel in one hand and a wet glass in the other, smiled at them and hummed, her eyes suspiciously glassy.

EPILOGUE

Maman had flown home to Montreal. The four of them were piled in JP's big bed on Sunday afternoon. Maeve and Angus had returned the kids about an hour ago, after taking them overnight as usual. JP had passed on football yesterday so he and Lucy could go out on their very first proper date, just the two of them.

Next week, JP thought they might combine football, a quick drink to introduce her to all the guys, followed by some precious romantic alone time. He thought that might work, long term.

Now, the four of them sprawled on his big bed, blissed out after a big lunch of grilled cheese sandwiches and tomato soup. Fifi snoozed between JP's legs like a rag doll, occasionally humming nonsense to herself. Lucy nestled against JP's shoulder while he slowly stroked her arm, occasionally pressing kisses to her sweet-scented hair. Along with the crumpled bed itself, she still held the warm scent of their night of hot sex mingled with shampoo, hair gel and the quintessential feminine smell that was uniquely

Lucy. He closed his eyes, inhaling and letting his breath out in a whispered, I love you against her ear, making her shiver and bring her shoulders up.

War of the Doctors played for the umpteenth time while they ignored the piles of laundry and toys, just drinking in the easy comfort of being together without pressure or worry or time constraints, floating on a cloud of happiness. JP read the paper, only half paying attention to the show.

Lucy's phone dinged. She groped, opened it, read some stuff. Rubbed her sleepy eyes.

"Huh. How do you like that?" Her face lit up as a smile stretched her lips, lifting her cheeks, bringing a bubble of lightness to his chest, lifting him even higher on this cloud of happiness he'd been floating on for days. He mirrored her smile, happy that she was happy.

"What is it?"

Fifi roused and crawled up between their bodies, nuzzling.

"I just got an email from Peter Sinnehauser. He's sent me an invitation to give a little talk at the book launch event up at the uni next week. He wants me to show the website and introduce Grandpa Henry and his work."

Their eyes met in a long, deep wordless conversation, all the shared events of the past two months swimming in the depths of their eyes.

He tightened his arm, squeezing her shoulders. "That's wonderful. Well-deserved, Lucy." JP bent to cover her mouth with his, putting all those thoughts and feelings into the kiss, trying to convey the embarrassment of joy and pride and contentment that filled his chest to bursting.

"He's hoping to meet me for a quick coffee later this

afternoon to discuss it." She looked up, reaching up to touch her messy bed head. "Ugh. I'd better go home and change my clothes. I look a fright."

Fifi sat up, crawling up Lucy's chest. She set her little hands to Lucy's cheeks, gazing up at her. "Yoofy pitty."

JP let out a guffaw. "I agree, Fifi, love. Lucy's very pretty, just as she is."

"Come with me?" Lucy's big brown eyes widened, and at his questioning frown, continued, "Please? All of you come?"

"Hmm. Well, in that case we'd all better get prettied up, eh kids? Wouldn't want your family to embarrass you at such an important meeting."

Did you enjoy this story? You can share the love by leaving a review on Amazon at amazon dot com/dp/1988743060 or Goodreads at goodreads dot com/book/show/53435345-single-dad-in-studio-7d

Turn the page for more books!

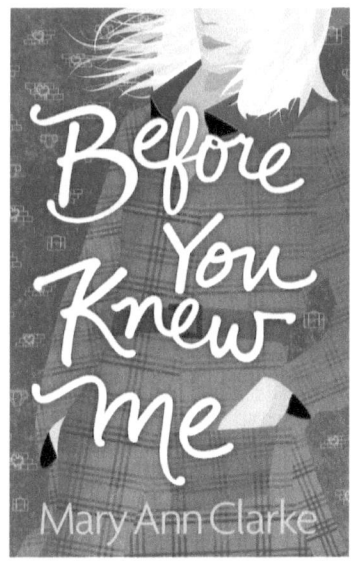

Pre-Order Now at books2read.com/BeforeYouKnewMe

Turn the page to read an excerpt of Before You Knew Me:

BEFORE YOU KNEW ME: HAVING IT
ALL BOOK 3

Chapter 1

Sharon Beckett ended the call and allowed herself a tiny
smug smile , opposing council's sighing words echoed in
her mind, *"You win, Sharon. Again. They accepted your offer,"*
as her gaze lifted from her sleek orderly desk to bask in the
sparkling twenty-second floor panoramic view of
Vancouver Harbour on this fine fall day. A fitting reward
for a job well done. And a glittering reminder of how far
she had climbed.

The art of war. It never got old. Another notch on her
belt. Fighting it out in court was fine, and she excelled at
that, too, in an efficient, controlled sort of way, but there
was nothing quite so satisfying as a neatly negotiated deal.
No mess, no fuss, every I dotted and T crossed. Her diligence paid off.

She stood, closed her laptop, straightened her Mont-
blanc pen in its stand, and grabbed her favourite coffee
mug with its bold black inscription, *You've Got This!*

Despite the visible reminders of her success, she needed this too. A daily reminder that she could. She *was* strong enough, smart enough. Good enough.

She eyed the dregs of cold coffee from earlier this morning, and strode to the door, a spring in her step. She had just enough time for a fresh espresso. It swung opened by itself, her associate Amber pulling up abruptly.

"Sorry! Heading out?"

Sharon lifted her brow in query.

"You won? You won!"

Holding back her smile, she asked, "What makes you say that?"

Amber flashed a toothy grin. "You have tells. You may not be smiling, but I can read you. Your chin is up, your shoulders back and you have that sharp gleam of victory in your eyes like an eagle."

A laugh spilled out. "I trained you well, Grasshopper."

Amber made a tiny curtsy of thanks. "Got a sec to review the Shin-Sao Foods case notes?"

"I'm meeting Meacham in ten. Perhaps afterward. Then we can go for a celebratory lunch. On me."

"Alright!" Amber spun on her high heel, punched the air and returned the way she'd come, down the hushed carpeted corridor of FSMBS. That girl would go far.

Snickering, Sharon carried her mug to the sleek black and chrome staff lunchroom and lounge that was a daily reminder of the classiness of her firm, and of how far she'd come. It was occupied.

His back to the door, fellow junior partner, Dariush Shirazi, worked the high-end coffee station like a professional barista, intently focussed, the scream and groan of milk foaming emanating from his mug. He neither heard nor saw her enter.

She stood a moment in the entryway, admiring the way his bespoke windowpane check navy suit fit his shoulders like it had been painted on. He and his stylish haberdashery had come from the UK a year ago to join the firm. He was a natural.

Shutting off the noise, and sensing her presence, he twitched and looked over her shoulder. Tossing her a flirty grin he said, "Hey, Sharon." His warm, appreciative gaze swept down and up again, reminding her of the low key interest he'd continually expressed since they'd met

With no flirty grin, she replied, "Dariush."

"Almost done here." The espresso dribbled into the cup, and she bit back a retort as he poured and stirred and sprinkled until he had arranged his fancy beverage to his fastidious liking. He was as delicious to look at as his decadent mocha caramel latte, but completely off limits. That was fine with her.

She rinsed her mug while she waited. Sharon had wasted enough of her life pining for Simon Sharpe and learned her lesson well. Success as an attorney came to her through diligence, but she was hopeless at judging the suitability of mates. It was just as well it wasn't on her agenda anymore.

The truth was, it gave her great satisfaction to know that she had earned the right to sit among the top legal brass, though the feeling of being an imposter never ceased. Despite already having her name on the letterhead, she was impatient to enter the inner circle and control her own fate.

Stepping away at last he leaned against the counter,

waving the way for her. She hit the button for a quick double espresso, which she'd barely have time to drink now before her meeting.

"Sorry to make you wait. What are you working on?"

"Starting a new *pro-bono* case for Meacham this morning," she replied.

He nodded with a silent, *Ahh*. "My sympathies. I'm sure you'd rather be slaying dragons. Will it be very boring?"

"I'll make short work of it." She shrugged, though she'd had the very same thought. She'd do anything for senior partner Arthur Meacham, even if it were boring. She wouldn't be here if not for him. He'd hired her right out of law school, despite knowing her history, knowing her father even. "You know, Dariush. If you're as interested as I am in making full partner, you might want to shift your perspective a bit. Community outreach, and public relations are important parts of this job."

He reluctantly acknowledged the right of it with a twist of his face, taking a sip of his coffee. After a beat of silence he cleared his throat. "Dare I broach the unpopular topic and again suggest we have dinner together? You can further enlighten me on the value of charity work."

"Ask all you like, Dariush. You know my policy. Hell would freeze over before I'd date a colleague never mind a fellow associate partner." She would never compromise her career here at FSMBS by doing something so stupid. There were rules. This position, her eventual, dare she think imminent, full partnership the thing she'd worked for all these years, never setting a toe out of line.

"You break my heart," he joked, yet she didn't miss the genuine disappointment in his dark gaze.

She smiled. "I don't doubt you'll find your one true love in time. You'll just have to look elsewhere."

She glanced at the wall clock and tossed back the remains of her espresso. "Time to go." Setting her mug in the sink, she spun and stepped to the doorway, then paused and turned back, a hand on the frame, feeling a twinge of guilt. "You know, Dariush, if circumstances were different..."

One side of his handsome mouth quirked up in acknowledgement as he met her gaze.

"You're a really great guy." Letting her gaze slide over his dapper form again with a smirk. "You're even my type. You'll make some woman very happy someday." She shrugged and left, her mind already jumping ahead to the meeting.

Sharon perched in front of Meacham's desk five minutes before the new client was due. In truth she was hoping if she sat staring at the fatherly old man, he'd give her a clue as to the nature of the project before they walked in the door, so she could mentally prepare herself.

Clearly Meacham had no intention of filling her in. Instead he calmly examined briefs while she sat stiffly across from him, observing. His eyes and cheeks were puffy, and she wondered about his health, and whether he was watching his diet. Then she frowned at the small succulent that sat on the edge of his desk, the lower leaves translucent and squishy. She'd given it to him last month, after a successful case, and tried not to read anything into its neglect.

She loved this firm, and had never wanted to work anywhere else. But pleasing Meacham kept her on her toes, and lately she had the feeling she wasn't quite measuring up, though in what way she didn't quite know. Despite what she'd said to Dariush, she didn't relish what lay ahead. Meacham seemed to think if she didn't make headlines with her charity work, it didn't count. She knew PR was important, but she couldn't help being introverted. And she wanted to make a difference without getting dirty and making a scene.

It ate at her, but she kept it to herself. Whatever lay ahead, she was smart, focussed, determined. She'd figure it out. *You're a winner. You can do this!*

Thankfully, Carrie knocked and showed them in right on time.

Two people entered. A middle-aged woman strode forward, and, back straight and shoulders squared, Sharon stood to greet her while her mind quickly took in pertinent details. She hadn't been expecting a corporate fancy. But this woman was extremely down-to-earth, in an inexpensive knitted tunic over black leggings and practical grey running shoes. Her salt-and-pepper hair was cut short like a man's, her smooth square tawny face unadorned by makeup. She wore a pair of wire-rimmed glasses over her sharp black eyes that gave her a professorial air. Crinkled corners belied her serious manner in the moment. This was a woman with wisdom and heart.

Meacham stood as well, his stern old face lit up with a genuine smile. Obviously the woman was an old friend and that's why he'd taken on her case.

"Christine, come in!" he boomed, clasping her hand between his. "Sit down. It's good to see you."

"Hello, Arthur," she said. "It's you who's being good, as ever. Thanks for doing this."

"Anything for you, my dear. Anything to help you in your ambitious work."

"Sharon, this is my old friend Christine Watts, with the Pathway Society."

Sharon's curiosity piqued, she offered her hand to the interesting woman and introduced herself.

"I'm giving you Sharon Beckett for the duration, and I know she'll do right by you and your organization, Christine. She'll leave no stone unturned. I trust her completely, and so can you."

That was news to Sharon, but she kept her editorial thoughts to herself. She couldn't help but feel this case was some kind of unspoken test. Nevertheless, she would do whatever was required, and she would do it well.

Christine murmured as she sat down, meeting Sharon's gaze with a small frown, "I hope it doesn't require too much of your valuable time, Sharon," and a tiny red flag went up. This was supposed to be a quick and simple favour, *wasn't it*?

Sharon was about to take her seat again as Christine sat when she noticed a tall young urban lumberjack in a hoody step silently up behind her.

She flinched and caught her breath. "Oh! Hello!"

"This is Kent Sawyer," Christine said. "He works for me, and he's been spearheading the project, so Sharon will work extensively with him when I'm busy with the kids, which is most of the time. I haven't the time to devote to the project that I would wish and still keep the operation running. But Kent is on top of everything."

Sharon stepped around Christine's chair and offered

her hand to shake, looking up, way up at his lean, broad-shouldered form, kicking the part of her sex-starved brain that heckled, *everything?* The sullen man merely inclined his head with a jerk of his bearded chin and a bare grunt of acknowledgement, not even removing the hands thrust into the front pockets of his wrinkled tan chinos. She frowned in concern and withdrew her hand. She'd be liaising with him?

He didn't look old enough to have a position of responsibility, never mind run a project. Was he some kind of student trainee? His hood shadowed his eyes, so all she could really see was his scowling mouth and scruffy brown beard. For whatever reason, he was profoundly unhappy to be here. Irritation radiated off of him in waves.

Sharon cleared her throat and slipped past him to drag a third chair over from the side of Meacham's expansive office, turning it and offering it to him. Kent. Kent Sawyer.

He mumbled his thanks, grabbing the chair from her to adjust its position before sitting, his long-fingers momentarily brushing hers before she could withdraw them from the chair's back.

His fleeting touch sent a jolt of electricity shooting up her arm, and she jerked her hand back, glowering at her knuckles in confusion, as though she'd been burnt. The jolt had not been mere static electricity, but something organic, cosmic and far more powerful, zinging through her nervous system and shaking her down to the soles of her feet.

She glanced up, curious, to catch his sharp amber eyes flickering to her face. Those striking tiger eyes flashed in recognition of the moment. He'd felt it too.

Like helpless jungle prey, her breath came fast and shallow. Her pulse raced, beating a drum in her neck. Her thoughts scattered.

She dropped her gaze, taking in his long legs to see that he wore an extremely beat-up pair of brown leather Blundstone boots. They looked like he'd worn them every day for a hundred years.

How could the mere touch of a man, an inappropriate, unattractive man at that, stir such violent excitement in her, instantly liquifying all her lady parts? He wasn't in any way the kind of man she was attracted to, as different from the dapper Dariush as night from day. He wasn't wearing a designer suit, for one. In fact he was poorly groomed. Maybe even unclean by the look of him. He had horrible manners and no discernible communication skills. And as if all that wasn't enough, he was probably a decade younger than her. She hadn't even got a good look at his face. She'd admired many a man in her day, crushed on a few, but never had she encountered one that rendered her speechless with pure unadulterated lust.

No. Just no!

She had standards, for one thing. And he didn't even come close.

Blinking, she stole another glance at his face to find his gaze still riveted on her face, staring back at her. Their eyes met, his intense golden brown eyes radiating both maturity and intelligence, as well as confusion and curiosity that matched her own, for a split second his angry scowl gone. This time the zing of connection hit her through their linked gazes sending alarm signals through her nervous system, triggering small explosions in her throat, chest and core. In that suspended moment, Sharon thought she knew him from somewhere, he felt so familiar. But instantly the scowl returned, his Adam's apple bobbed, he nodded curtly and turned away to sit.

Well, at least he wasn't quite as young or as dull-witted as she'd originally thought. But who or what was he, exactly?

She sat, mentally shaking herself to bring her focus back to the meeting. Christine was already talking to Meacham and Sharon couldn't afford to miss a single nuanced detail if she was going to do this right.

Even if she had to work with *him*!

End of Sample. Buy now!

THE **ART** of
ENCHANTMENT

MaryAnn Clarke

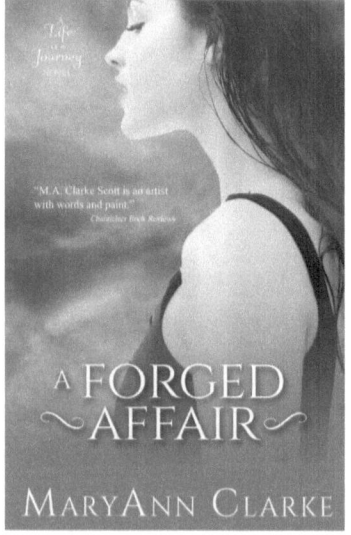

A **FORGED**
~**AFFAIR**~

"M.A. Clarke Scott is an artist
with words and paint."
Chandusley Book Reviews

MaryAnn Clarke

MaryAnn Clarke is a Chatelaine Grand Prize winner and Next Generation Indie Book Award finalist for The Art of Enchantment, first in the Life is a Journey series about young women on journeys abroad who discover them-selves and fall in love while getting embroiled in someone else's problems. Her Having it All series is about profes-sional women struggling to balance the challenge and fulfillment of their careers with their search for identity, love, family and home.

Always eager to fill blank pages and empty canvases with ideas swirling in her head, MaryAnn set out to write emotionally engaging stories that walk a tight rope between intelligent Women's Fiction and heart-warming Romance.

A polymath who studied Fine Arts, Urbanism, Architecture and Gerontology at university on both coasts of Canada, she turned to her first love, writing stories, when she realized she could have more fun with fewer rules to follow as an author, than working in an office as an architect, or in a university as a researcher. When not writing, she meditates while hiking wooded mountain trails, does yoga and Pilates to fend off decrepitude, reads eclectically, contemplates wormholes, experiments with painting abstract expressionism, kills plants and tries not to burn dinner while solving her next plot problem. Now that her chick has flown the coop, Clarke lives on beautiful Vancouver Island, Canada with her husband and cats. Although she knows she lives in Paradise, she still loves traveling the world in search of romance, art, good food and new story ideas.

Stay in touch to hear book news, special deals and updates about next release- Before You Knew Me, Book 3 in the Having it All Series. You can always reach MaryAnn at maryann@maryannclarkescott.com

You can read more about MaryAnn, her books and ideas that strike her fancy at www.maryannclarkescott.com.
    WANT TO READ THE LATEST BOOK IN THE LIFE IS A JOURNEY SERIES?

BUY ON A FORGED AFFAIR ON AMAZON :
mybook.to/Forged

WANT TO CONNECT WITH ME?
www.maryannclarkescott.com
maryann@maryannclarkescott.com

If you enjoy reading this book, please rate it and leave a review on Goodreads HERE. Your opinion can make or break an author's success, and it means the world to me. Go here to leave a review: https://www.goodreads.com/book/show/45285118-single-dad-in-studio-7d

Subscribe & Follow MACS!
www.maryannclarkescott.com
Question? Fan mail? Sure, you can reach me here.